The Time After 2012:
The Mayan Sunset

MATTHEW B. THOMPSON

ISBN-10: 0988540525
ISBN-13: 978-0-9885405-2-1

DEDICATION

To my wife, my mother, my sister, my brother, Steve, Kate, Marge, Arliss, Ryan and Zack. You have all encouraged me more than you realize.

CONTENTS

CONTINUED

ACKNOWLEDGMENTS

I am very grateful to wife, Lori, who guided my thoughts and helped me edit the book. I am also grateful to my professional editor, Dawn Boeck, who was able to dedicate her time and effort to helping me complete this book. I also want to deeply thank English teachers I had in Junior High School and High School. They were constantly in my mind as I typed.

I used several elements of American Pop Culture, including creations of George Lucas, Steven Spielberg, Melissa Matheson, Michael Grais and Mark Victor. Another bit of American Pop Culture are the many brand names under Kellog's. Finally, a multitude of Google's features were extremely helpful in writing this book.

It's helpful to read the glossary first. (Uncommon words.)

In 1916, Woodrow Wilson promised the American people that he would keep America out of the war in Europe. Once elected, though, he took America INTO that war and tilted the European balance of power. Prior to that time, only Europeans had shaped Europe. After the war, Wilsom-influenced politics destroyed the German economy and guaranteed 2nd World War which would require an ultimate weapon. Without Wilson's 'fib', the German economy would not have been devastated, the Nazis would not have risen to power and the Weimar Republic might still exist. There would not have been World War II, the Holocaust, the nuclear bomb or any of the other nuclear programs in the world. An old proverb talks about the road to hell... and how it's paved.

Chapter 1

The Battle Of Los Angeles

(February 25, 1942)

Sitting at a console on the front-left side of the small craft, the young helmsman turns his head slightly to speak, "They're firing at us, Sir." Undisturbed, he turns back to the screen.

An older man with a neatly trimmed white beard and white hair sits forward in his chair. Sitting behind the helmsman and in the center of the small vessel, he stares at the forward view-screen. A third man, a communications officer, sits in the rear. "I'm amazed they even know we are here," he says, his deep voice resonating. His deep blue eyes on the forward view-screen. He doubtingly asks, "They have weapons that can reach us?"

"Yes, Sir," says the handsome young man. "Effective ones. They'd bring us down if we were hit." Blue eyes, blond hair, clean-cut and slender; even though he looks to be only 20 years old, the handles himself like a veteran.

"They've made amazing progress since my last visit, Percival," he says in a low voice. "Just evade," he orders. "We don't want to hurt them," he says. "Maneuver: Pidima. The bouncing maneuver will work just fine."

"Yes, K'kul," he answers and presses a few buttons.

Sitting behind the older man's left shoulder, the young communications officer chimes in, "Sir, we are receiving a message from L'lith's ship. Text only."

The older man sighs loudly and rubs his forehead like he has a headache. "Yes?" he asks quietly.

The communications officer reads the text, "We have detected strange radiation signatures and are investigating further."

K'kul takes a deep breath then says, "Break formation and head toward the main ship. Tell them that I am coming aboard."

The small vessel maneuvers away from the two dozen other silvery vessels, then silently flies toward a dark form, a very *large* form, hovering in the darkness. Beginning the landing sequence, the sensors come to life and reveal every detail of the dark form in front of them. A circular ship isn't unusual to Percival, even if it looks like a giant Tesla Coil, but the sheer *size* of the ship never ceases to amaze him. Knowing the exact dimensions does not make the scene any less incredible. The blue and black mottled pattern covering the top and bottom sections constantly changes, like it is a living creature. The middle section is dark gray in color and completely flat, allowing for landing bays and other storage areas. One bay opens its twin doors and a welcoming blue light appears.

Percival automatically plots a course toward it. The view-screen's image grows and grows as the small vessel approaches the giant ship, like an ant walking up to a watermelon. The small vessel slips past the twin doors and blue signal lights, revealing a massive docking bay. Without a second thought, Percival maneuvers the craft into the cavernous docking bay and the welcoming blue lights change to become 'unavailable' red lights. Tall and slender, K'kul stands and impatiently waits for the craft to land. The instant the small craft touches down K'kul steps through the doorway and disappears through the door.

K'kul stomps into a conference room with three men and a woman standing in front of a large view-screen hanging on the wall. A table sits in the middle of the room. Even from behind, he recognizes each of them instantly. The four immediately stop talking, like it had been a private conversation that he shouldn't hear. Ignoring their silence, "What's going on, L'lith?" he bellows.

A stunningly beautiful woman turns her head to face him; her long red hair brushes her shoulders lightly. K'kul averts his eyes. "'Hello' to you, too, K'kul," she replies quickly.

He purses his lips, forces himself to be calm and politely asks, "What did you find?"

"We were waiting for you," she tells him. Her draping maxi skirt brushes the floor. Split in the front, the overside is black while the underside is blue. A long cape runs to the floor, again with a black overside and blue underside. Two of the men seem to revive from a trance while the third, a very tall and muscular man, lurks near the woman. K'kul looks at the three men, "R'ma... M'kul... P'al...good to see you."

Slender and handsome, the two normal-height men radiate intelligence and strength like sunshine. R'ma has black hair, wearing an olive green tunic with gold details and M'kul has shoulder-length blond hair, wearing a bluish tunic with white details. P'al, the giant, has short-cropped brown hair and a chin goatee, wearing black battle armor and a long black cape with a blue underside, similar to the woman's.

She walks slowly toward the view-screen. "As I said, I was waiting for everyone to arrive first." The view-screen comes to life on it's own, displaying technical data and charts. "We detected a strange radiation coming from one of their cities."

Unmoved by either her beauty or her delays, "And?" K'kul asks impatiently. "What is it?" he demands.

Ignoring his irreverent tone, "They are making plutonium," she says flatly. Speechless, the four stand in silence like they'd heard the news of a friend's death. K'kul slowly backs up and sits at the table.

Anticipating his next question she calmly says, "We're sure. The scans are conclusive." The others stand in silence, as if at a funeral. Emotionless, she sits at the table while her words seem to echo through their minds. The others follow suit, as though waiting for her cue. The silence echoes through the room for several moments.

Shaken, one man quietly says, "We knew their technology would advance quickly, but I didn't think they'd advance *this* quickly."

"None of us did, R'ma," K'kul says. Then to the woman, "Is it coming from Los Angeles?"

"No," she answers. "It's from further up the coast."

"We can't monitor on them every thirty years anymore," K'kul insists, "It has to be done sooner now."

"The more we interfere with their progress, the more we shackle them," the blond man says.

"They are advancing much faster than we expected, M'kul," K'kul counters. "Our nets are too wide. They're spiraling."

"Are they spiraling downwards or upwards?" she asks.

K'kul shoots a look at her, "Technology and wisdom must keep pace with each other," he tells her. "If technology outpaces wisdom by too much, then the society will spiral downward... rapidly. It always does."

She scoffs. "Then *give* them wisdom," she answers.

M'kul says, "Understanding comes with experience. Failure and success *can't* be taught."

R'ma ignores the squabble, pushing the topic aside. "Plutonium has only one real use," he says. "We should monitor them yearly and prevent the other side from developing more serious technologies."

Shocked, M'kul exclaims, "Yearly?"

K'kul bellows at the same time, "Neural omissions again?"

R'ma answers both men, "Solar years, M'kul, not lunar ones. K'kul, no need to just to conclusions. This is not Heron or Aristocles all over again. We'll use a simpler and much more palatable strategy."

The woman cuts in, "These people are becoming more and more connected to each other. They spread their knowledge before we can get to them. Neural omissions are no longer effective."

Silent until now, a deep and guttural voice asks, "Destroy it again?"

"No," K'kul answers, "That didn't work in 1912. They found a way around it. L'lith is right. This world is becoming smaller with each passing year."

"Yes," R'ma adds.

K'kul continues, "If we allow them to continue this project, it will stop ITSELF."

M'kul doubts him, "How do you figure that?" he asks.

"This is an ultimate weapon," he answers matter-of-factly. "If no one else can counter it with something more advanced, they'll win the war and this whole thing will end."

"Exactly," R'ma nods. "We'll allow this technology and stifle any others."

"They are clever," M'kul mutters. "Damn clever."

"Yes, they are," K'kul answers. "Burying their creation under three miles of water wasn't enough last time. Instead of destroying their creations, we should simply TAKE their creations," he says. "They can't fix things they can't find."

"That includes Foreign National crashes," R'ma adds. "They're already headed for another technological revolution, but we don't want it to go too far."

"Agreed." M'kul interjects. "We need to assign men to blend into their society and constantly monitor them. Men in black, so to speak."

"We only need one person for this," the woman says. "If we just move him from place to place, people will think there's a lot of them. That'll also keep our fingerprints to a minimum, while keeping 'Control' to a maximum. We'll recruit a human from the *other* side of this war, someone very familiar with all the new technologies. Does everyone agree?" She looks around at the nodding heads.

K'kul graudgingly says, "Yes." He stands, opens the door and walks drudgingly through it. He reappears at the small vessel fifteen minutes after he had left. Disappointed, he orders, "Take us back, Percival."

Startled by the instruction, he spins his chair toward K'kul, "Sir?" he asks.

"Something's happened," he says. K'kul walks slowly across the cabin and sinks into his chair. "The Council has decided to wait... and I agree. We'll let this situation calm down and try again later... much later."

Knowing not to ask, the young man quietly says, "I see." Spinning his seat back toward the control panel, the silvery vessel silently lifts off. He solemnly steers it between the massive bay doors, then back down and under the dark water.

The Long Count of the Mayan calendar predicts celestial, human and even mystical events with uncanny accuracy. The calendar mysteriously ends on December 21, 2012. Astronomers say the end of the calendar is simply an annual alignment with the center of the galaxy. Modern Maya aren't sure but hope for peace. Christians and others are afraid of the rise of the Antichrist or the Apocalypse. No one knows the answer.

Chapter 2

70 YEARS LATER...

December 19, 2012
(Long Count of 12.19.17.17)

In an Internet chat room.

Tex: What do you think, Asher?

Sitting at the computer to eat, he shifts his plate of food over to get to the keyboard.

Asher: I dunno.

Asher: It seems strange that people are thinking of this whole Mayan thing as the looming Apocalypse.

Asher: I hadn't really thought about it until

```
                         just now.
```

Sarcasm doesn't work well in a chat room.

```
Joe:       Really?  You hadn't thought about it?
Joe:       I know you're dying to tell us, so go
           ahead.
```

The three have been chatting on the Internet for nearly two years. Even though they all live in Washington, D.C., they've never met face-to-face. Tex got his nickname from living in Texas and Joe came from 'G.I. Joe' because he is a medic in the U.S. Army, but Asher's nickname had not been as inventive - it's just his last name.

Asher's face flushes. Luckily he sits safely on the other side of a computer screen.

```
Asher:     Since you really want to know...
Tex:       Come on.  Let it out.
Asher:     The  Maya  lived  a  thousand  years  ago
           and    were    a    highly    advanced
           civilization in Central America.
Asher:     They   had   a   super-accurate   calendar
           that was even more accurate than ours.
Tex:       See?  YOU feel better we're DEFINITELY
           better.
Tex:       You're   done   since   we're   all   better
           now.
Joe:       Very funny, Tex.
Joe:       But I want to hear more about it.
```

Joe: I like stuff like this.

Tex: And once he gets started it's hard to
          shut him up.

Asher ignores him.

Asher: OK.   It's probably sounds a bit
          geeky...

Tex: No! You?

But adds before anyone explodes.

Tex: Sorry. Sorry. Couldn't help it.

Asher: Their calendar did more than just
          count the days.

Asher: They got information from previous
          civilizations   for   eclipses,
          hurricanes,   earthquakes,   births,
          deaths and other stuff.

Asher: They   found   regular   cycles   in
          EVERYTHING and put that in their
          calendar,   then   used   it   to   make
          predictions.

Asher: That type of thing is geographic
          region-specific.

Joe has a moment of brilliance...

Joe: You would think that San Francisco or
          New York could do the same thing.

...and then it's gone.

Joe: Is this what Nostradamus did?

Asher: Nah.

Asher: Nostradamus wrote a bunch of vague
          stuff, then took credit for it when
          something happened to fit.
Tex: Like that astrology crap.
Joe: I don't know what you guys are talking
          about.
Joe: I follow my horoscope every day.
Tex: You would.

Ready to pounce:

Joe: AND WHAT DOES THAT MEAN?

Asher interjects, hoping to calm their tempers.

Asher: Nostradamus' real name was Michel.
Tex: Mike? That's cool!
Asher: No.
Asher: Michel, pronounced like the girl's
          name Michelle.
Joe: He was a girl?

Asher laughs to himself.

Asher: No.
Asher: Michel is a traditional boy's name in
          France.
Tex: That figures.
Tex: Hundreds of years later, he's STILL
          screwing with people.
Tex: I guess the French version of a badass
          soldier believes all that crap, too.
Joe: I'm a medic, not a soldier.

Joe: But I guess reading isn't your strong
         suit.

Desperately trying to defuse the situation:

Asher: Michel de Nostra-Dame flunked out of
         medical school and changed his name to
         'Nostradamus.'
Tex: Okay, I'll bite.
Tex: Why did he change his name?

Relieved that he finally distracted them, Asher eagerly
writes:

Asher: So no one would recognize the name of
         a flunky.
Asher: He ran around the countryside, calling
         himself a doctor and selling magic
         potions.
Tex: Didn't he write, too?
Asher: Vague stuff, yeah. It's called 'Cold
         Reading.'

Joe jokingly writes, getting in the conversation again.

Joe: Reading a book in the snow?

Asher-the-egghead answers the question without missing
a beat.

Asher: It's a technique for reading a person
         without knowing anything about them.
         Cold.

He realizes it is a joke as soon as soon he hits the 'Enter' key.

Asher: Speaking of snow, when are we going out on the town?

Asher: I just can't do weeknights.

Tex: Government worker.

Tex: I thought you government types could come to work whenever you want.

Asher: It doesn't work that way in MY office.

Asher: It was at your suggestion that I go get the job.

Joe: We're both happy for you, Asher.

Joe: When we first started chatting, you were just using that big brain of yours to write computer programs in your parent's basement.

Joe: Now you're on your own and working on computers in the White House.

Asher: It's the Eisenhower Building. They're easy to confuse.

Tex: Whatever.

Tex: We're trying to give you a compliment.

Asher: Oh. I'm sorry.

Tex gets annoyed.

Tex: That's what we've been talking about.

Tex: Even though you've moved out on your own and gotten a great job, you still lack one major thing...

```
Tex:     confidence and assertiveness.
Asher:   You know that's two things, right?
```
Tex explodes.

```
Tex:     Dammit!  That, too!
Tex:     Quit being so damn... literal!
Tex:     People don't like it and women REALLY
         don't like it!
```
Joe breaks in so Tex can calm down.

```
Joe:     Just be assertive, have confidence and
         quit correcting people.
Joe:     That's all you need to do.
```
Asher sits back, thinks for a moment, then writes:

```
Asher:   I'm not sure if I want her to remember
         me or not.
Joe:     Joanne?  Are you still thinking about
         that one girl?
```
He hangs his head.

```
Asher:   I'm trying to improve myself for lots
         of reasons, but she's what I use as a
         gauge.
Tex:     He's obsessed.
```
Asher rockets out a response.

```
Asher:   I am not!
Asher:   I see her opinion as a high mark on
         the 'female opinions gauge.
Asher:   If I pass her inspection, then I'll
```

```
               pass ANY inspection.
Tex:     That's probably true.
Joe:     I'm not sure how high a mark it is.
Joe:     All she asked is that you don't live
         with your parents, have a job and act
         like a man.
Tex:     On the first date?!
Tex:     I can understand on the third, seventh
         or even the twentieth date.
Tex:     But on the FIRST date?!
Tex:     I agree with Asher.   The  girl's  a
         snob.
Joe:     Okay.  She asked a lot of him a bit
         too early in their relationship.
Tex:     What relationship?!
Tex:     That was their FIRST date!
Joe:     Fine!  Fine!
Joe:     The girl has issues.
```

Elsewhere in the World

In the pre-dawn hours, the thunderous roar of a jet engine echoes across the desert. "Cruising at 36,000 feet. Smooth as silk," Major Donnelly says on the radio.

"Continue on course three zero six," a woman's voice answers. "We'll be glad to see you two back."

Another man sits directly to his left, "After 31 hours," he says, "you should be ecstatic. "Have you heard anything from my wife? The 'due date' is almost here." The white sands and towering dunes glint below them. A pink horizon hints of the coming dawn.

"Negative, Colonel," she answers. "But I will call and ask. These things can be a bit unpredictable."

Out of nowhere the cabin shudders. "What the hell?!" Colonel Drake yells. Alarms sound throughout the cabin and the shudder becomes a violent upheaval. "Strap in!" he yells. Major Donnelly catches a glimpse through the window. As if in slow motion, he sees the horizon twist to the left, then up to the sky. The violence swells into a tidal wave of ferocity, as if a massive earthquake has hit the aircraft. An invisible force shoves the two men back into their seats. He looks at the control panels. "The port wing's been hit!" he yells. "The computers are trying to compensate! I don't think it'll go!"

Colonel Drake yells at the radio, "Something's hit our port wing, but from above!"

"Meteor," the radio says. "Eject!"

The G-force pulls hard. The Colonel grunts from the force. "Not happening!" he manages. "End over end! We're going down!"

Sitting in front of a white tent and a campfire, a young Bedouin man watches the early morning sky. A black dot catches his attention. As it grows larger, he realizes that it's an airplane. "Muhammed!"

An older man stumbles out of the tent, "What? Where is breakfast?"

He points at the falling airplane, "Look!" he says.

Muhammed stares at it for a few moments then smiles, "An American airplane." Ecstatic, "Everyone out!" he yells. "Now!" Several men slowly walk out of the tent. "This is our chance, my friends. Allah has smiled on us. That," he says, pointing to the falling airplane, "is an American airplane. It's black because it is one of their secret airplanes. Much, much gold!" Electrified by their luck, the group can hardly restrain themselves. Steadying the group for a few more seconds, "We must capture it and anyone inside," he tells them. "The men are worth much more if they are alive. Let's go!" he yells. "Allah is with us!" The men rush to their camels, yelling in excitement.

Several Hours Later

Focusing on the transponder's blip on a small screen, an American helicopter pilot talks on his radio, "Sir, the transponder says it's here, but I don't see anything at all." The mid-twenties pilot wears sunglasses and a camouflage uniform while flying above an endless ocean of sand dunes.

The raspy electronic voice of an older man answers, "It's not like the damn thing's small, Captain." The helicopter pilot could hear a sigh over the radio. The rough, older man's voice continues. "But maybe something's broken off or hidden in the sand. In a sandstorm, things can be completely buried in minutes."

"Understood, Sir," the young pilot answers, both acknowledging his superior and finding solutions to his superior's problem. "I'll set down and have the team fan out. We'll find it." As an afterthought he adds, "Sir, this isn't very encouraging for the colonel and the major."

"That's already crossed my mind, Captain," the radio answers. "Just find them!"

The pilot lands the helicopter and relays the orders. They offload, carrying metal detectors and transponder locators then start the search. "Colonel," the young pilot says over the radio, "We ran into a Bedouin group a little while ago. They seemed agitated, but I figured it was because we're soldiers in a helicopter."

The Colonel scolds him. "That PC crap will get you killed, Captain. More importantly," he adds, "it can get our men killed."

The helicopter pilot subconsciously hangs his head a little. "Yes, Sir," he answers and quietly sighs.

Outside the men focus on the side of one sand dune. "Sir!" one of them yells. "We found the transponder signal and large metal object!"

With more pep in his voice, the Captain relays the news on the radio, "Sir, they found the transponder signal and a large metal object."

"Good, Captain," the electronic voice tells him, "With the way they went down, we don't know if they were able to eject."

Digging in the sand, the men uncover the black nose of the airplane. "We got it!"

The men quickly uncover the window. Sgt. Aaron whips out a flashlight, scanning the cockpit's insides though the front window. "I don't see anyone inside, Sir!" he says.

Another soldier has been uncovering the top of the cabin. "Sir, I don't think this was buried by the wind," he says. "The door's been opened, I don't see anyone inside and some parts are buried deep while other parts are buried shallow. I think this was intentional."

The chopper pilot head-smacked the air in front of him. "The Colonel was right," he says to himself, "It was the Bedouin group." He leans out of the chopper and yells, "Aaron and Smith! Stay here and guard the aircraft! Don't uncover any more! The rest of you, climb in!" He revs the helicopter while four men clamber aboard. The two guards shield their eyes as the blades blow a mini-sandstorm.

"How do you want to do this, Sir?" a soldier asks, yelling over the screaming blades.

The pilot didn't like being fooled by such a simple trick and turns his head halfway to talk to his men, "Simple. I'll drop three of you off a few hundred yards away. Peretti, you'll stay here and translate for me. The two of us will land and make a big deal. While they're distracted you three will go in, find the men and get them out the back. We'll give you about 20 minutes then pick you up." Getting angrier by the minute, "These primitives may have found it," he says, "but I guess they thought we'd actually let them keep our equipment." He turns forwards and the helicopter lifts off. He mutters to himself, "Or our men."

The law 'All U.S. residents will receive free and appropriate education' has been applied to many things. This has increased lawsuits against the schools, lawyer fees and school system abuse by administrators... and parents. All of that increases school expenses and therefore school taxes. Only childhood education and parental involvement have decreased. If failure of a public school course resulted in the student paying for the course, education and parental involvement would increase while expenses would decrease. Like it or not, financial risk motivates people.

Chapter 3

December 20, 2012

(Long Count of 12.19.17.18)

"Stella!" he screams.

Appearing near the man's ladder, as if summoned by magic. "George, you know that my name is 'Kim."

"I know," he says, smiling and laughing to himself. "Kim Hunter."

She crosses her arms. "Yeah," she says indignantly. "How do you get 'Stella' from 'Kim?" she asks.

He answers, "Kim Hunter played Stella Kowalski."

"Was that some cop show back in the 80's?" she asks sarcastically.

He sighs, mutters something about kids these days and climbs down the store's stocking ladder. "Doesn't matter," he says. "We'll need to stock this whole aisle again".

She suddenly notices the bare aisle. "Oh my god!" she says. "What did they do with all this stuff?"

He sarcastically answers, "They bought it."

Ignoring him, she walks partway down the aisle. "I stocked this entire aisle YESTERDAY!"

"Yep," he says nonchalantly. "Partly it's Christmas-time," he says while walking through the stock room doors. He comes back with an enormous teddy bear under each arm. "Partly it's this whole 'Mayan baloney,' he says while moving his arms or as much as can carrying two giant teddy bears. After arranging the new bears with the last one on the shelf, he goes back to the stock room.

"What's all the excitement about anyway?" she asks.

He looks at her, "First of all, it's about you watching me work."

"Sorry," she says and scurries to the stock room to get more stuffed animals.

When she returns, he authoritatively continues, "Well, the old calendar of the Maya ends in a few days." He picks up a five-foot nutcracker. "I'll get these, and you get a couple more bears." He mutters to himself, "Morons. Our calendar ends *every* year."

"Why is the big and expensive stuff going so fast?" she asks.

"This also happened in 2000," he says, carrying the large nutcracker through the door. "The Apocalypse-people think the world's going to end, so they buy big gifts for Christmas. They probably think they won't have to pay for them." After stocking the shelf, they arrange it. George walks back into the stock room and yells back at Kim, "It's good for business, though." Picking up another soldier, he trods back to her and says, "I feel sorry for those grocery store guys, though. Their customers buy loads and loads of Pop-Tarts and beer!" he laughs. He gets more and more amused, saying, "I mean… Do these people actually think that Pop-Tarts will save them?! I guess if Pop-Tarts don't, the beer will take the edge off!" He laughs even harder.

In A Catholic Mass

Some parishoners are half-asleep from last night's party when a gray-haired priest shouts, "The 'End of Days' is upon us!" Many people sit up. *It might be just a knee-jerk reaction,* the priest thinks, *but at least NOW they are now paying attention.* "St. Malachy warned us of this. In 1139, he prophesied that the last pope, the Antichrist, Peter the Roman, would be the 112th pope... misleading the 111th pope with his beautiful, yet *poisonous* words. Beginning with Pope Celestine II in 1143, the current pope, Pope Benedict XVI is 111th pope. The Bible tells us that after has already reined for seven years, the Antichrist will reveal himself and then *destroy* the Catholic Church." He pauses, letting the words sink into the minds of his parishioners. The people murmur and shift in the pews.

"His coat of arms," the priest continues, "'*De Gloria Olivae*', 'The Glory of the Olive', could refer to 'The Order of Saint Benedict', his namesake... or it could refer to him as the "Bringer of the Olive Branch', a peacemaker... or he could fulfill 'Olive's Glory' as revealed in 'The Mystical Eschatology of the Vatican' and returning 'The Keys To The Kingdom To Christ's Second Coming'. Prophecy *necessarily* lacks details."

The old priest becomes silent and bows his head. "The Antichrist is sinister," he says at last. "We all know this; it isn't a new idea." He pauses again. "Most people think that means 'evil,'" he says. "'Of course, he's evil' we all say. 'He's the Antichrist!'" He put his hand under his chin. "Does that mean evil or does that mean left-handed?" he asks. The parishioners murmur again. "Or both?" he adds. "Sinister, smoke and fire, foreign-born, European ideas, talks about the olive branch..."

"But there is hope; Christ can *only* come after Antichrist has reigned," he tells them somberly, "and Pope Benedict's coat of arms has two large keys hidden in the corners. The Antichrist is smart. He knows we know these secrets. His rise may be a *boom* or a in a whisper - we don't know which, but we do know that this pope served the Nazis. Will he bring peace to the world or will he lead us into the clawed hands of the Antichrist? The Antichrist is *cunning*. Do not assume the answer... but don't ignore the obvious, either."

At The Same Time

A man wearing a blue shirt and khaki slacks walks into an office at a university in the state of Arizona. Another man, dressed in a dark-colored suit and red tie, barely notices the man enter as he thumbs through papers on the desk. "Mind if I have your apple?" the visitor says. He looks up, but before he can answer, the visitor snatches the apple from the desk and bites into it with a loud *crunch*.

"Yeah, sure," he says sarcastically and continues looking at individual papers, then puts them in his satchel. "I don't see why it's such a big deal, Richard," he says, "It's just an alignment."

"They want to make sure the sun will come back," he says and bites into the apple again. Noticing all the papers on the desk, "Grading papers?" he asks. "No T.A.?"

He puts the last of the papers into his satchel. "This isn't an eclipse and no," he answers, bustling toward the door, "We found something strange on some satellite images, so I'm taking the printouts home. I hate to run out on you, but…"

"Press… I know. Just remember that reporters are like wolves," he says. "When they're young or from a distance they're kinda cute, but up close and grown up, they'll rip you to shreds and eat you alive."

He stops for a moment at the door, "I doubt it's that bad," he says.

"Maybe not… but maybe so," he says. "They're not stupid, but they're not the sharpest knives in the drawer." Dr. Livingston hurries down the hall. Richard walks to the doorway and shouts, "I bet you ten bucks that they ask about dinosaurs and California."

Shouting from the end of the hall, "Okay, you're on!"

Outside

The head of the Astronomy Department, Dr. Bill Livingston, stands amongst microphones and speaking to cameras, "This is nothing more than an alignment," he tells them, half-blinded by camera flashes. "The Earth and Sun have aligned with the center of the galaxy every 26,000 years and has done so for four and a half *billion* years. That's more than 173 thousand times. The Earth is still here." The reporters did not seem to understand.

In the frenzy, a single person calls out, "I thought it was 640,000 years."

Bill smiles, thinking, *This will be easy.* "You've been watching too much TV. The Ancient Maya believed that the center of the galaxy was the birthplace of mankind," he tells them. "This probably symbolizes a rebirth of some kind, but certainly not the end of the world. That's Christian ideology, not Mayan." While the reporters fought each other, battling to get their question heard, he hoped for an intelligent question. No such luck.

A man's voice eclipses the others, "Dr. Livingston, what about the dinosaurs?" he asks. "Didn't an asteroid destroy their world, but not the planet? How is that different?"

Dinosaurs, he thinks. *That's not BOTH things*, so *I don't owe him ten bucks just yet*. "It's true that an asteroid helped to destroy them, but it's also true that we have been cataloguing and tracking objects like that for decades, for exactly that reason. We know the exact position and path of the every large object crossing Earth's orbit."

"Candace Cohen from the *Tulsa Gazette*," another reporter announces. "Most objects, yes, but not all," she adds to his statement. The reporters hush for a moment then mumble amongst themselves.

Amazed that she was able to shut up a reporter feeding frenzy like this, Dr. Livingston decides to try a softer approach with her. "You're a long way from home, Ms. Cohen," he says, smiling. "Asteroids hit each other all the time, sometimes sending one our way and sometimes breaking off chunks. We aren't in the business of assuming that we know the location of every rock in space, just like you wouldn't assume a geologist knows the location of every grain of sand on Earth. However, he does know where all the beaches are located, and we do the same kind of thing. Big asteroids are the dangerous ones, but those are easy to track. Earth is in no danger."

The reporters squabble amongst themselves for a few moments. *Why would anyone want a life like that,* he wonders. A single reporter appears to ask her question. "Dr. Livingston," she says. "What about California? Can this event push it into the ocean?"

Dammit! he thinks. *She HAD to bring up California!* "I'm an astronomer, not a geologist, but my understanding is that the tectonic plates are grinding along each other, not away from each other. California's *never* going to fall into the ocean and certainly not because of an alignment."

"So as a non-geologist," she says, "you can't say 'For Sure', can you?"

She has completely wasted her life, he thinks. *And after watching a few TV shows even believes she's a top-flight attorney.* He'd like to slap this woman for spreading her stupidity, but knows that HE would be the one is trouble. Instead, he grits his teeth and answers, "No."

For the believer, there's an overabundance of evidence.
For the non-believer, there's never enough.

Chapter 4

The Return of the Nine

December 21, 2012
(Long Count of 13.0.0.0.0)

At exactly 6:55 in the morning, a circular mass rises from the depths of the Catalina Channel near Los Angeles. Water doesn't even touch the bulbous object as it silently slips from the ocean's grasp. The brown circle grows larger and taller, looking like a giant turtle shell. The turtle shell grows into a brown *mountain*, like the ocean is birthing the horn of a new continent. The horn is a *titanic* UFO, climbing through the waves. It escapes the watery slumber without splashes, bubbles or even a hum. Released from the sea, the immense craft levitates skywards, a swirling vortex of water churning briefly beneath as it leaves. Short and thick 'wings' encircle the titanic spaceship. Suddenly, two pale white engines ignite on one side, lurching the mountainous ship forward and toward the City of Angels.

At a nearby military base, a blip appears on a radar screen… a very large blip… moving very quickly across the screen. "Whoa!" the radar operator says out loud.

The other tech in the radar room sits only a few feet away in the small room. Without taking his eyes off of his own computer screen he asks, "What's up?"

He jumps off his stool and points to the screen. "You've gotta get over here and confirm this!" he yells at the tech.

Irritated, he says, "Hold your horses. It's not like I'm a mile away." He walks over and looks at the screen. "Whoa!" he yells. "Confirmed! Get the C/O on the line!" he yells. "We've got a bogie nearly on top of us!" Moments later, and a dozen miles from land, two F/A-18 fighter jets patrolling the skies get a radio call, changing their orders. They immediately change course and ignite their afterburners.

The leviathan reaches Long Beach in only a few minutes. It changes course and moves toward the famous area of Hollywood. The F/A-18's reach the leviathan before it gets there. The commander flips a few buttons and radios the tower, "Secure transmission to General Westin."

A supremely confident voice comes over the radio, "This is General Westin. We're secure, Commander."

"Sir," he says, "This is not your typical bogie. Look at my forward camera, and you'll see what I mean." He transmits the image.

A few moments pass before the commander hears, "Holy Mother of God!"

"Sir," the RIO interjects, "This thing is as long as three aircraft carriers and moving like greased lightning!"

Commander Eppes tells him, "Sir, I don't think SAMs or ACUs can keep up with this thing. We're gonna need a LOT more fighters up here."

General Westin takes a deep breath. "Commander, I'm going to send every available fighter I can muster. You'll have a small army in a few minutes. We won't lose it this time!"

Commander Eppes and his wingman fly cautiously behind the leviathan, trying to hide their presence until reinforcements arrive. They don't have to wait long. Within two minutes and from several directions F-16's, F/A-18's and even F-4 fighter jets join them. Fifteen aircraft strong now, they move up and buzz around the silent craft like angry hornets. Minutes later, even more fighters arrive to challenge the leviathan. The hulking ship lumbers past the city, changes course to the southeast, then heads into the desert. For a split second, the fighter pilots think they've won a small victory. However, they soon realize that the monstrous ship's new direction is taking them directly to Las Vegas!

Three planes quickly fall into an attack position behind the huge vessel. They fire a barrage of bullets above it as warning shots. To no avail. Commander Eppes radios back to base, "We fired warning shots over the ship with no response. It's broken deeper into U.S. airspace and presents a clear and present danger. Do I have permission to fire my missiles?"

General Westin's voice appears, "Commander, as soon as you are in an unpopulated area, you have permission to fire."

"Yes, Sir. We are nearly there now," he answers. He swallows with difficulty, "We're over the mountains now. Jared and Rogers, prepare to launch both of your sidewinder missiles." He says a quick prayer. "Now!" he screams. Six sidewinder missiles detach and scream toward the ship. In an instant the leviathan jumps to 5,000 miles per hour.

Stunned at first, Commander Eppes watches as six smoke streams harmlessly trail off into the clear sky. "Holy crap," he whispers. Getting angry, he rumples his face. *Son of a...,* he thinks. After a few *choice* phrases to himself, he speaks normally on the radio, "No joy, Sir. The bogie jumped to an astonishing speed before missiles could even reach it."

Captain Jared breaks in, "It bolted like nothing I've ever seen, Sir! There wasn't even a sonic boom. That's not even possible, Sir."

The steely general orders, "Pull back for now, boys. I've already radioed Las Vegas. This isn't over."

Near Las Vegas

Five F-22 Raptors fly in a clear blue sky over the Nevada desert. "This is not a drill, gentlemen," the lead pilot says. "Our airspace has been deeply penetrated by a hostile force. Set your weapons to hot. Permission granted by General Westin. RJ, do you see anything on the radar, yet?"

"No Sir," he answers.

"Keep your eyes peeled, Captain," he says. "We're flying straight into them. General Westin said that this thing was moving like greased lightning; and that's no joke. Ground-based radar clocked this thing at over 5,000 knots."

The captain puffs out a small laugh, "Colonel, at those speeds our onboard radars won't be able to track them for more than a few seconds. We need a ground-based feed." Then suddenly, "Whoa, Sir! Bogie at two-seven-one!"

Colonel Bratten doesn't hesitate, "All aircraft, fire your missiles!" Time moves slowly as Captain Watson watches ten smoke plumes scream toward the leviathan. The giant ship seems to jump out of the way for an instant then back to its original course. He blinks his eyes. "Go to guns!" he yells. Just as they start to fire, the leviathan flies straight into them. It seems to jump around as it did before, leaving five aircraft completely unscathed and completely alone.

"RJ, did you just see that?" he screams. "Did you have the video recorder on?"

"Yes Sir, I did... on both counts," RJ answers. "Ground has a live feed." Never more than 3,000 feet above the ground, the leviathan heads straight toward the desert oasis that is Las Vegas.

In A Casino Hotel Room

From a hotel room window, a sleepy woman watches the rising sun on the desert's horizon. Still dressed from the night before, she watches at the desert's dawn. Suddenly, the giant ship streaks in front of her pleasant scene and *instantly* slows to a crawl. Her eyes bulge. She blinks them a few times before looking again. She still sees it… slowly moving toward her. "Chuck!" she screams. "CHUCK!"

"What?" a man groggily answers from the couch. "I've been up all night. Drinking and gambling and whatever else I did. What do you want?!"

She beckons him with her hand, "Come here! Quick! There's a Star Destroyer outside."

More awake now, "What?" He stretches, gets off the couch and lumbers to the window. "I've been awake all night, got drunk off my ass and even came over here to see your hallucination. Now what the hell do you want me to see?" he asks. The leviathan reaches the hotel, blocking the entire horizon and passes overhead. "HOLY CRAP!" he yells, instantly awake. They both drop to the floor. They huddle together as a giant shadow passes over every hotel in sight. "That was *not* a Star Destroyer," he tells her. Five fighter jets suddenly appear and streak across the sky on full afterburners. Chuck whispers to her. "That was only the first one," he says. "The military is involved and can't keep up. We just saw the scout ship for an alien invasion."

In Other Parts Of The Country

Denver, Lincoln and now Chicago try different attack strategies; each assault more dangerous and more deadly than the last. Even though missiles are not effective against a target moving at such extreme speeds, they are better than nothing. Fifty, a hundred, two hundred jet aircrafts from across the country join forces to fight the titanic intruder. No two planes look alike, but they fight alike. Jet aircrafts launch barrage after barrage of missiles and bullets, but the massive ship does its bouncing maneuver and simply evades the American 'clouds of death' like they're not even there. The intruder never fires a single shot, dodging the bullets and missiles and simply continues flying toward the Windy City as if nothing has happened.

News reporters, film crews and citizens film the incredible scene as the massive ship flies overhead. "I can't believe it," a woman tells a reporter on camera, "I can't believe this is really happening. God help us!"

A man jumps in front of the camera. "*Now* do you believe us?" he asks. "We've been telling you that they're coming for *years*." The woman puts her face in her hands and sobs. "You didn't believe us then. Do you believe us *now*?!" the man shouts.

Television stations around the world interrupt their programs to break the news of a possible alien invasion. "The American military, the world's strongest military, seems powerless to stop them. We've even heard rumors of a nuclear attack."

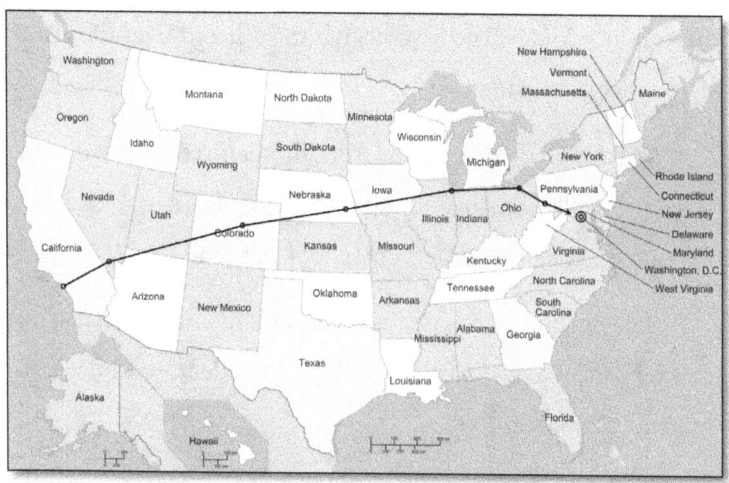

In The White House

A young soldier runs up to a general about to walk in to the Oval Office. Saluting the dark-skinned man, he says, "Cleveland failed, too, Sir. They've jumped to hyper-speed again. If they skip Pittsburgh, they'll be here in about four minutes."

"Thank you, Son," General Hamilton tells him, salutes and walks through the door.

The room is filled with people talking loudly, and all at once. They hush for a moment when the general comes in, anxious for the news. "Cleveland's failed, gentlemen," he tells the others in the room, the noise immediately resuming. "We have four minutes," he says, trying to be heard over the crowd. The room gets louder.

A white-haired man, dressed in a dark-colored suit and a blue tie, walks up to him. "Alan, how did it go?" he asks. Obviously agitated, he nervously looks around.

The general stands at attention for a moment, salutes, then relaxes and says, "Not well, Mr. President. Almost two hundred fighter aircraft..."

General Hamilton's words fade as the president unexpectedly sits down and talks to himself. "Not good! Not good! I didn't want this job," he mutters. "I mean the perks are great, but..."

The general interrupts his rambling, "Sir, we still have two methods of attack." People in the room must have heard him because the noise calmed down a bit.

The president snaps out of his stupor for a moment. "Okay," he says.

"Mr. President, their speed has rendered most of our weapons useless… but not all of them," he says. The crowd hushes a bit more, listening intently for a ray of hope.

"Okay, go on," he says, more interested.

General Hamilton remains standing. "Sir, we have laser detonators. They're kind of like large ray guns," he says, stretching the truth a bit. "These are mounted on humvees and the beams travel at the speed of light. They can't out-maneuver lasers. It'll take them down."

"Oh wow!" he says, standing up. More confident now, "It sounds good, General. Let's get those boys going."

"They're already being deployed, Sir." More stoically now, "Mr. President, there is another solution." The room hushed into an eerie silence. General Hamilton lowers his voice to just above a whisper. "As a last resort, Sir, we can detonate the device once they reach us."

President Harwell remembers. "Ohhh," he whispers. "I'd forgotten about that," he says under his breath. Gritting his teeth he looks down. "Damn," he says. After a few moments he looks up again. "Well let's hope the ray guns do the trick," he says. Smiling and even giving the general a friendly punch on the shoulder, "I don't think this dog's going to bark."

"No, Sir," General Hamilton cautiously says, astonished by the change.

A non-uniformed man comes up to the general and salutes as best he can. "At ease, Son. You're not a soldier."

Relaxing a bit," Yes, Sir," he says. Only then noticing the president, he straightens up again. "Mr. President," he says. Medium height, thin, pale and in his mid-twenties: The guy had probably spent most of his life in front of a computer screen. "Radar telemetry shows that they are not flying on a direct course."

"That's obvious," General Hamilton says with irritation.

"Yes, Sir," he answers, "But it appears to be flying across large populations while moving in this direction. It slows down to a few hundred miles per hour over these cities and its altitude has never been higher than 3,000 feet."

The general's irritation becomes an almost-restrained anger. "We already knew that!" he bellows. "Why are you here?!"

The man seems to shrivel, "We don't think they're going to attack."

Stunned, "What?" President Harwell asks.

The man swallows. "They fly low and slow over large populations, obviously wanting people to see them. Un-armed people that they could easily destroy. They fly across the entire country rather than drop straight down from space. They're taking the long way around by showing themselves to lots of people, which exposes them to attack. Then they choose to evade those attacks, refusing to engage our fighters. Something's up, Sir. They seem to want everyone to know they're here and that they're coming to see you." He looks at President Harwell.

President Harwell realizes what this means, says, "Oh crap!" and sits down again.

General Hamilton shoots a look to the pale man. "Dismissed," he says quietly. The pale man walks away.

He sighs and sits next to the president who is now sitting and hunched over, saying, "Crap!" over and over again, under his breath. He looks up at the general, "It's one thing if they're going to destroy all of us. It would be really bad, but at least our suffering will end at some point. They're after me! ME! Personally! Who knows how long they can…" He trails off and winces at the terrors and tortures his brain has created. Jumping back into the conversation, "And they're going to be here in four minutes."

The general seems to want to cheer him up, but remains formal. "I hate to tell you this, Mr. President, but it's two minutes now, Sir."

"Oh God!" he cries.

"Mr. President," the general says in a stern whisper, "Get ahold of yourself! The people need you, Sir. Now more than ever before."

Immediately inspired, President Harwell sits up straight, "You're right, Alan." He straightens his tie and stands up. The general also stands. "'The only thing we have to fear is fear itself.'"

"Mr. President," the general says, "He could easily be wrong. Low and slow over large populations could be psychological attack, terror tactics, not friendly aliens."

The president straightens his tie again. "I am the President of the United States and this is a diplomatic situation," he says.

General Hamilton straightens his body, almost standing at attention. "Mr. President, it is my duty to present you with strategic facts and possible courses of action. This is an extremely unusual situation and you need real strategic alternatives - not the hopeful stories of Hollywood."

"I understand," he says, "and it's appreciated. But these aliens are exposing themselves and have gone out of their way to prevent a battle, even when we fired first. There's a good chance for a peaceful meeting."

President Harwell changes his tone. Until now, he had been talking with the general like a friend to a friend. Now he speaks to his like a boss to an employee. "Get as many of the laser cannons as you can get. I want them on the White House lawn by the time that thing gets here." He speaks very precisely and very clearly. "*Do not fire* any unless I give the order."

"What if you are incapacitated, Mr. President?" the general asks.

He starts to walk out the door and says, "Then I don't care. Do I?" General Hamilton gives him a 'serious' stare. "Just kidding," the president says. "The vice president can decide what to do." He stops at the doorway, smiles and looks back, "I feel much better now." He turns and walks out of the room. Bellowing down the hall, "They'll be here in less than two minutes, people! Let's get ready!"

The general spots the CIA Director. He had been lurking nearby. "This is all over the news," he says, waving his hand.

"There's nothing secret about this," the general tells him, "so why are you here?"

Avoiding the question, the director leans toward the general and says, "He's the one that got rid of the other guy, you know. Of course he wanted the job!"

Incensed, "Allegedly," General Hamilton snaps... then dutifully follows the president.

The Big Bang Theory states that the entire universe began as a giant explosion... a bang. Although the vast majority of the other galaxies are moving away from the Milky Way, a few are moving toward it and explosions simply don't work that way. Another tidbit is that scientists can't account for ninety-four percent of the universe. They say neutrinos or dark matter or dark energy or something else causes it. All the bandages in the world can't turn a wrong answer into a right answer. There are even more tidbits.

Chapter 5

Pidima

General Hamilton walks into the Situation Room to find the president looking at digital footage on a 20-foot video screen, following the giant ship's movements. A red line connects the cities that are highlighted with red circles. The general walks across the room and stands next to the president in front of the huge screen. The line connects Los Angeles to Las Vegas to Denver to Lincoln to Chicago to Cleveland to Pittsburgh. Washington D.C. has two red circles. Green circles highlight Detroit, Indianapolis, Columbus, Cincinnati, Philadelphia, Baltimore, Boston and New York City.

"They've paused over Pittsburgh," the president says to the general. "That gives us a little more time."

He already realizes that, but says, "Yes, Mr. President."

President Harwell continues, "I figure that this is as good a place as any to wait for the inevitable."

General Hamilton took a breath, "That's true, Sir. We can watch its movements very well in here."

The president turns to face someone else, "Zoom in," he tells a tech. The huge screen immediately zooms to show a 300-mile radius around Washington, D.C. Seconds later an arrowed red line begins to move again, rocketing toward Washington.

"Damn, it's fast," President Harwell tells the general. "That trip is nearly an hour by air."

"Yes, Sir," the general replies. "They are moving at about 5,000 miles per hour. Only the *Aurora* can match that speed."

President Harwell turns his head and looks at him, "The what?" he asks.

The general's face becomes blank and rigid, "Nothing, Mr. President." General Hamilton says. Still feeling the president's stare on the side of his face. "I was talking about the Aurora Borealis, Mr. President."

President Harwell turned back to face the screen, chuckling. "You military guys have a strange way of looking at the world." General Hamilton chuckles aloud while silently breathing a sigh of relief. *This president is a breeze,* he thinks to himself.

The president looks at the tech. His pale face seems to glow behind the computer screen. "What do you expect they'll do once they arrive, Mr. Asher?" President Harwell asks him.

He looks up for a moment, unsure that he'd heard his name at all. He sees the president's gaze and immediately becomes excited, thinking, *The President of the United States knows my name!* He tries to keep his excitement in check, but a slight grin escapes. He wipes the grin off his face as fast as he can. With all the authority he can muster, "They'll probably hover overhead for several hours," the young man answers. Feeling a bit more certain, Asher adds, "That is a really, really big ship, so they'll need to send down a shuttle." The general discretely clears his throat, signaling the tech. "Mr. President," Asher hastily adds.

Pleased by the news, President Harwell smiles. "We have more time than we thought!" he says. Asher almost says something, but General Hamilton puts a finger to his lips, signaling for Asher to be silent. "I'm starving," the president says. "Who's up for pasta? I'll have the kitchen fix some," he says as he walks out of the room.

General Hamilton dutifully follows him again. "Not a word to anyone," he quietly tells Asher as he walks out of the room.

"Yes, Sir," Asher says quietly. Alone in the room and alone with his thoughts, replaying the last few minutes in his mind, Asher kicks himself. *Joseph Harwell is the President of the United States of America and NOT one of my buddies. He deserves more respect than I am giving him,* Asher tells himself. *He's the most powerful man on the planet,* he thinks... then adds, *At least he was. I need to make a much stronger effort.*

In The Streets of Washington, D.C.

A vast and mysterious shadow silently crosses the Capital City. A dusk-like twilight covers dozens upon dozens of city blocks in every direction as the massive ship's partial-shadow engulfs them, bringing streetlights to life. Seconds later the midnight-black umbra reaches them. Sunlit streets turn into inky black coffins in mere seconds.

Confusion becomes panic. Sheer panic. People realize the alien ship is not just passing by, it's coming *here*. They scream unnaturally and shout profanities at the top of their lungs. Panicked birds screech profanities of their own, but the enormous ship makes no sound at all... even at only six hundred feet in the air. Car horns blare, tires squeal and metal smashes into metal. A mother pushing a stroller suddenly stops and covers the slumbering infant. She screams, "Oh, my God! My baby! Help my baby!"

News journalists broadcast the event while the leviathan finally comes to a halt directly above the White House. Visions of disaster, a major disaster, pound the minds of millions of people.

President Harwell watches the event on a portion of his massive video screen then runs to a window. "My God!" he yells. "It's even bigger than I'd imagined," he tells the people in the room. "It's one thing to hear the numbers. It's quite another to see it for yourself." Stretching from the Grand Hyatt to George Washington University to the Tidal Basin, the monstrous machine hovers over the entire, sprawling city, barely above the top of the Washington Monument. President Harwell turns back to the video screen in time to see a tiny craft launch from the giant ship. Cylindrical and silvery, the tiny ship seems to float down to the South Lawn. Turning to Asher, the president asks, "Can't they beam down or something?"

The pale man proudly answers, "Mr. President, that's the shuttle I mentioned." He feels more of an authority than he did a few moments before. He continues, "Sir, *beaming* is more of a 'TV & movie magic thing' than something real. There's been quite a bit of research on that subject, Sir, but..."

President Harwell cuts him off. "You also mentioned that they'd hover for hours," he tells Asher. "They're hovering alright. Hovering a shuttle to our doorstep! I'd say you're only right half the time!" Filled with testosterone and adrenaline he turns to the general, "General, are those laser blaster things in place?"

"Yes, Mr. President," General Hamilton says. "On your order."

Alarmed, Asher jumps in, "Mr. President, it's only one out of three times."

President Harwell didn't realize he was still there. "What?" he asks absently.

"If they were hostile, then why did they send only one shuttle?" he points out. The president and the general stop and listen for a few seconds. "If they're friendly then there'd be no reason to wait. It's likely that the shuttle has very important people on board... possibly the most important people they have."

General Hamilton jumps in, "Why would they send their leader on a recon mission?"

Asher answers him as plainly as he can. "It's not recon, Sir," he tells him and then explains, "If it's a 'friendly situation,' there's no need for recon." Asher has never felt so alive! His opinions are altering the course of an entire nation, perhaps the whole planet. "Look above you, Sir," he tells the general in a quiet voice. "They have the equivalent of a fleet of warships surrounding us. How much more safe could their leader be?"

The general quietly says, "It could still be psychological warfare, Mr. President." Turning to face the president and straightening his uniform, "But Asher's right in that we shouldn't fire on the shuttle." The general discretely signals the president this time, saying, "I still recommend that we keep the other option in mind, Mr. President."

President Harwell doesn't seem to understand at first. "Oh yeah!" he suddenly announces in a room filled with people. "You mean the b..." The general shoots an imploring look at him. The president stops talking and looks around. "Device," he whispers.

Just as tightened nerves seem to loosen, the same soldier ran up to General Hamilton. He salutes and says, "They're landing now, Sir. South Lawn."

General Hamilton says, "Thank you, Son," and salutes to dismiss him. As the young man quickly walks away, the general turns and says in a low voice, "Mr. President, I think we should get you into the room the Secret Service designed for you. The Safe Room."

President Harwell looked like he'd just woken from a daydream. "What?" he asks absentmindedly. "And you actually think that'll work?" he asks sarcastically. "Do you think that would prevent an armada of aliens from finding me and vaporizing me?"

The general tries to correct himself, "Mr. President, I only meant..."

The president cut him off, "Don't worry about it, Allen. Nerves are short right now."

Asher jumps in, "Mr. President, I think it'd be a significant gesture for you to walk out there to meet them."

Both the general and the president look at him like he's crazy, "You have *got* to be kidding," the general says. "Son, we've tolerated…"

Asher cuts him off. "Sir," he says, looking at the general's reaction for a split second. "There is an alien armada above our heads and possibly their leaders in our backyard. We are beaten. The best course of action is diplomacy."

General Hamilton sighs loudly, purses him lips and says, "I hate to admit it, Mr. President, but he makes a good point." He straightens up. "Diplomacy is always a good option and … as much as I hate to admit it, we have been beaten," he says, mumbling the last words. "I *really* don't like the idea of you walking out there by yourself, Mr. President, but I'd consider it an honor if I came with you."

President Harwell smiles, "I expected that you would." Both men walk out the door and toward the back of the White House with various people stepping aside to let them through. The general opens a door to the South Lawn and sees the silvery ship on the ground, about 100 yards in front of them. One or two people cling to the porch, but the area is otherwise vacant. What began as a clear and sunny day, now feels dark, windy and cold. As the pair begins to approach, colossal lights under the massive ship ignite, bathing the entire South Lawn in daylight.

General Hamilton smiles, "I guess they know you're here," he says. He can now see that the silvery craft is just a seven-foot tall silvery cylinder. He thought the ends were flat, but can now see that the ends are very slightly rounded. Looking like a giant soda can, minus the paint, the mysterious ship is only 15 feet long with no windows at all. They walk carefully toward it. Each footstep is a step into the unknown… and tension builds with each one. President Harwell's eyes refuse to blink, and he has to keep reminding himself to unclench his hands. About 20 yards away there is a hissing sound. Both men stop. Part of the silver craft's side seems to melt away, leaving a perfectly shaped doorway and re-forming into stairs; each step of the stairs hovering in mid-air. President Harwell's pulse seems to stop as a foot emerges, landing on the newly formed stairs.

Located entirely within the Antarctic Circle, with the wind slowly blowing in a vast circle around the continent, make Antarctica much colder than it's northern counterpart. Only a few animals and some lichen can call it 'home,' making Antarctica the most lifeless continent on Earth. Barren, nearly lifeless, no active geology, eternally frigid and yet a mystery remains. Most of the ice is less than 13,000 years old. Why is that? Shouldn't it be millions of years old? What happened 13,000 years ago?

Chapter 6

The Others

The foot becomes a leg and the leg becomes a man... a *human* man, descending from the silver craft's steps. The president and the general relax a little. The human-alien has blond hair and wears silver and white clothing, similar to a Karate Gi. Holding a dark brown spear-like device about five feet long in his right hand, he steps down and onto the grass, but remains expressionless as he stands near the stairs. The general wonders about the weapon. Green eyes stare blankly at the two men. Suddenly another foot appears from the craft.

The first man seems to come to attention as an older man appears from the craft. Having gray hair and a neatly trimmed gray beard, he wears light gray clothing that looks something like a suit. He immediately approaches the president, stops and bows his head slightly. Speaking in a deep baritone... and in English, "Greetings from Atlantis!"

Completely and totally stunned, the president immediately turns to diplomatic etiquette. "I am President Joseph R. Harwell and this is General Allen Hamilton, my Joint Chiefs of Staff Chairman. We are pleased to meet you." He carefully extends his hand.

The bearded man looks at the president's hand for a moment then grasps it. "We are also pleased to meet you," he says. "I am G'brael, leader of the Atlantean people and this is S'lon, my guard and assistant." S'lon nods, but doesn't divulge any emotion at all. "We have been waiting for this opportunity for many, many years."

President Harwell relaxes a bit more. "We have heard of Atlantis, but I never took it to be any more than a myth," he says.

"The island of Atlantis sank long ago, and the underwater city built later has the same name," G'brael replies.

Genuinely interested, the general tells him, "Admittedly, I have a strong interest in our culture's old legends. I always thought the two cities were the same thing."

G'brael smiles, "Not at all. 'Atlantis' is the name of the first *human* city built underwater. We named it the same thing as our old city as a symbol. Over time, the name became synonymous with 'underwater city,' but seven more cities were built... and none of them are called 'Atlantis,' either." He smiles again, like he just made a joke.

His mouth hanging open, General Hamilton manages, "Eight cities? Alien cities on Earth?"

G'brael nearly laughs, "They're not aliens. They're Lemurians, the first sentient species to evolve on Earth!" He looks above and behind him, "And here they come!" A second silvery craft, identical to the first, quietly makes its final approach to the president's left. Neither man had noticed it.

"Such stealth is frightening," General Hamilton tells the president in a low voice as the silvery craft comes to rest on the grass. The president nods in agreement. The technology in front of them is *far* more advanced than anything America has ever produced.

G'brael turns his gaze away from the second craft to tell the president, "They built the first two underwater cities. Our people have worked closely with their people since the ocean swallowed our first city nearly 10,000 years ago. I'm pretty sure you're safe." He smiles coyly and turns back to the second craft.

It lands and the door melts away, just like the first. The president holds his breath. A small foot steps onto the newly formed stairs. The general maintains a solid look on the exterior, but his heart is beating so hard that it feels like it will rip straight through his chest. The foot becomes a leg and the leg becomes a short, grayish alien with big, black eyes. Another immediately follows him... or is it her? Only 3 ½ feet tall, both are dressed in dark gray, slick-looking uniforms, like some sort of jumpsuit. Their skin is light gray, but still gray... and those eyes! Those big, solid black eyes! They stick out like an ant's head... a giant ant's head. Those gray aliens don't even have a nose! Just three grooves where a nose should be. They didn't have antenna, six legs or clamping jaws, but they look some kind of ant person. One of the gray creatures walks up to President Harwell, who is completely stunned with fear. Then looking to G'brael, they say something that sounds like a bass guitar playing Morse Code. "Yes," G'brael replies. "They've come alone. Our sensors prove it." The small creature turns to face the president.

"President Harwell," G'brael says, "this is a Lemurian... 'Achoo'."

The president and the general fight the urge to snicker. "I'm sorry," President Harwell says. "Did you say his name is 'Achoo'?"

G'brael sighs. "Yes, I did," he says. "And the other one's name is 'Ditz'." The president and the general fight the urge to burst out laughing this time. With obvious effort, he asks, "How did you understand him?"

"I can understand any language," he replies. "Even gibberish. I'll spare you the details, but I have a ring implanted around my brain that allows me to sense what the person *intends* to say, which completely bypasses language. It's a different area of the brain from language. Actually, it's several areas." He traces his fingers from the very top of his head and to the back, near his neck. "The ring is a circular antenna that faces forward when I look at someone and tells my brain what he means to say. It controls my lips and tongue to produce the correct language while building up a database of the language. I know the language anyway, but I would speak English because *you* speak English. The same is true for any other language."

"Why don't you just wear the ring on your finger?" President Harwell asks. "That would keep you away from major surgery!"

G'brael fights the urge to snicker this time. "It's not that kind of ring," he says. "And there's no surgery involved. We use a series of injections that become solid once they are inside the body." He moves his fingers around his head again. "The ring is larger and encircles your brain." Lowering his hands, "It does quite a bit more than translation," he says. "We used to wear them on the outside of our heads. We gave one to King Solomon of Israel." Asher's ears perk up. "It was called 'The Ring of Solomon' for a long time, but I think your people call it something else now. You might need one when you meet other species. President Harwell's stomach knotted for the hundredth time today. "Lemurians were the first sentient species on Earth," G'brael continues. "They emerged from the Arthropods nearly 500 million years ago and reached sentience 300 million years ago. They don't have tongues, so can't speak English or any other human language. Human cultures, as different as they seem to be, are remarkably similar. You'll see what I mean when you meet some of the Foreign Nationals."

President Harwell's mood immediately switches from amused to apprehensive. "What did you say? Genuine aliens?"

G'brael explains. "They are alien to your world. Yes. But not much more than a Japanese man is alien to the United States of America. They eat, sleep, breathe air, are born and die. They are Foreign Nationals and don't live here. They trade with us like you do with Japan."

Feeling a little more secure now. "Are they slimy and telepathic with tentacles?" he curiously asks.

G'brael laughs again, "Not at all," he says. "None of them are slimy, telepathic or have tentacles. No creature can operate electrical equipment if it's slimy. It will electrocute itself and short out the circuit in the process! What you perceive as telepathy is actually radio. Some robots are built so that you can't tell whether it's a robot or not. S'lon is an android." The president and the general look over at S'lon, but he simply nods again. They stare at him intently, but still can't tell. They give up and G'brael continues, "They signal each other with radio, like two people talking on walkie-talkies. As for the tentacles: It's true that some aliens have them, but they are all animals that live on an alien's home planet, like the octopus lives on Earth. Tentacles are very good at enormous amounts of strength as well as incredibly fine manipulation, but it just doesn't happen out there. Most sentient creatures have two arms, two legs, one head and stand upright. Those characteristics are the most effective for developing high levels of technology in the first place."

Inside The White House

General Hamilton escorts President Harwell, the two human-aliens and the two Lemurians into the White House. Several people sit around a large table in the main conference room. Asher, the main technical assistant, is included as well. General Hamilton opens the door and everyone stands. President Harwell walks in, stands behind a podium and announces to the room, "Please stand up... I mean continue standing for four men... creatures... I mean visitors. They come to us from the underwater city of Atlantis. Please help me welcome G'brael, S'lon and our small friends, the Lemurians. We know them as the Grays. The President and everyone politely clap as the two humans enter the room. The clapping softens and slows as the Lemurians enter the room. People that are closest to the door back away a little.

When most of the clapping had stopped, G'brael leans to President Harwell's ear, "Lemurians are not Grays."

President Harwell looks up at him, confused. "But they're gray," he says. "They have big head and black eyes."

G'brael smiles. "There are *several* species of gray aliens in the galaxy," he says. "That's like saying a Mexican and a Egyptian were the same thing since they both have brown skin and brown eyes." He pats the president on the shoulder. "You'll see what I mean when you meet the Foreign Nationals."

G'brael starts to move to the podium, but President Harwell stops him and nervously asks, "How... how many more are there?"

G'brael pauses. "We trade with 23 planets," he says. "As for how many more are out there," smiling devilishly, "that's for you to find out for yourself." G'brael smiles and pats him on the shoulder before walking away.

The Lemurians climb into chairs at the conference table like a small child would do it. Their chins reach over the conference table, but just barely. Their large heads and black eyes make them look like frogs sticking their heads out of the water while their legs barely reach the end of the chairs' seats. Although they are the size of small human children, several people standing close to them slowly back away. G'brael stands behind the podium and addresses the room, "I have an announcement!" The room isn't loud, but grows quieter anyway. "There is a reason we flew over some of your most populated cities the way we did. There is a reason why we refused to fire at your open hostility. You have grown out of your adolescence and there won't be any more secrets. Video of this meeting is being broadcast around the world as we speak and interruption of alien communications is stopping right now. This is the fifth and *final* Commencement of Mankind. You are one of us… and we were the gods of your ancient world. You are more advanced and more powerful than you realize. A new era begins today and it is time to begin to take your place in the galaxy."

He starts to walk away from the podium, but stops. "The biggest secret will be the most difficult for you to believe. I know that serpents have drilled and drilled the opposite thought into your heads, but… HUMANS AREN'T STUPID," he announces, emphasizing each word. He pauses for a few moments, allowing the words to sink in. Continuing, "In fact they are the smartest life forms in the entire galaxy." Again he waits for his words to sink into people. "Many of you might think that this doesn't apply to you, but you'd be wrong. Earth is the MIT of the entire galaxy! Just make it through elementary school here and you've beaten 99% of the galaxy. Think about it like this," he explains, "A computer built in

1950 versus one built in 2010. The 1950 model is much slower, but has been doing things for *sixty years*. It designed the SR-71, ran Apollo, sent men to the moon and designed every computer built after it. The 2010 model is much faster, but hasn't had time to do much. It doesn't need the extra time, though, because it's almost caught up. Lemurians gained sentience and have been doing things for 300 million years. Humans gained it only 50 thousand years ago and haven't had time to do much. You are the latest models in the galaxy. You don't need extra time, because you've almost caught up already."

A few people seem to grasp the gravity of what he is telling them, but only a few. G'brael speaks softly for a few moments, "You are so close... so very close... and you don't even realize it. One of your brethren once said that any sufficiently advanced technology is indistinguishable from magic. How many things are explained with 'magic' today? " His words create a stir in the room. "When you go see a magician, do you say, 'He's really magic!' or do you ask, 'How did he do that?'" The people mumble to each other. "Wouldn't that mean that you are so advanced that *nothing* is considered 'magic' anymore?" He smiles, like a proud father smiles at his child, "That doesn't mean things aren't beautiful or special. That just means you don't use the word 'magic' to explain the unknown anymore. You are almost grown up now. Technology is merely a convenience. Nothing more. It's *far* more important to organize yourselves well. Fundamentals are not very exciting, but they are quite powerful. You are a collection of individual people, not a collection of interchangeable parts. Remember that. The sheer power of a true individual is astounding. You will truly impress yourselves with your own ingenuity. Communism and socialism are merely survival techniques. If they are used on a large scale for more than a few years, they *destroy* individuals. Not all at once and definitely not instantly. Leaders can only speed it up or slow down the process. They're not the *real* problem... bureaucracies are. Don't get me wrong. Some bureaucracy is necessary, but it needs *far* more size-management than anything else. Most of them need to be downsized out of existence - reduced to an absolute minimum then cut them in *half*. Only after you do those things will you begin to taste freedom again."

"We built a few things for navigation, but *you* built all the other amazing monuments on this planet ... all by yourselves. Serpents will try to convince you otherwise, but 'No.' You did them yourselves. Self-reliance is your *most powerful* ally, but a good teacher needs to impart a few fundamentals every now and then. There IS a God. We have *physical* proof. You were *never* cavemen. You are our children. Marxism kills FAR more people than it saves. There was no Big Bang. The universe is a LOT bigger and a LOT older than you think it is. There is *no* Higgs Boson. There are *eleven* dimensions of space-time, not three or four... and they are all, quite literally, in the palm of your hand. False beliefs like these and others have impeded your people for more than a century. Fundamentals may not be exciting, but they *are* the answer. Remember that and you will make up that century in a decade. You once called us gods then angels. Now we want you to call us friends. You are our sons and daughters... and you are more clever than any other Commencement of Mankind has ever been. We will see you again in our home. Until then, we bid you a very fond farewell." With that, G'brael steps down from the podium.

Some people applaud while others shout: "What?," "Where are you going?," and "But we need you." The people applauding G'brael stare at those shouting. They drown them out with applause in a standing ovation.

G'brael tries to walk past President Harwell and toward the exit, but he grabs his arm. "Where are you going?" President Harwell asks.

G'brael stops. "We are going home," he tells him.

"Have we offended you in some way?" President Harwell asks.

"You haven't offended us at all," G'brael replies. "In fact, you've beaten every other Commencement by more than two and a half millennia. That's why we didn't stop your spreading across the entire globe. We couldn't be pleased with you more."

President Harwell looks like a child begging a parent. "But we need you," he pleads.

G'brael looks at him and smiles. "You need us as much today as you did yesterday." G'brael pats him on the shoulder and says, "Remember what I said. I know your people can do it all by yourselves." He reaches for the door handle when the door opens.

A beautiful red-haired woman walks though it instead. "Maybe they don't want to jump through your hoops, G'brael," she says.

G'brael's eyes show his shock, "L'lith!" He immediately turns his eyes away from hers. The Lemurians look up in horror. "It is not your place to come here, L'lith," he tells her, growing more and more angry. "You were never invited."

Wearing a black skirt, bodice and cape with blue, leather pauldons, she smiles coyly and seems to glide into the room.

"You forgot to invite me, G'brael," she says. "One might think that you didn't want the Americans to know there were other opinions out there."

G'brael's face grows red, but manages to keep his voice under control. "That's not it, L'lith." Gritting his teeth he adds, "and you know it."

When L'lith moves toward the conference table, the Lemurians slide off the chairs and run for the door. "I never liked them anyway," she mutters. She turns around and leans against the conference table. Her cape is black on the back, but blue underneath. The skirt parts in the front, revealing the blue underside, just like her long cape. Long, black leather boots complete her sleek wardrobe. She announces to the room, "I am L'lith, leader of the Osirian City-State. It's one of ten city-states built under Earth's oceans."

Breaking in, "Two are Lemurian and one no longer exists," G'brael says.

She ignores him. "From an *unbiased* perspective," she says, "I see you swooping in here, dangling your toys in front of their faces and then leaving. Where have I gotten it wrong?"

"I wasn't dangling anything," he says. "I told them who they are, and gave them clues…"

L'lith immediately cuts him off. "Clues? Clues?! For crying out loud, G'brael, these are your children! Give them more than just clues! You're a teacher. Give them a spaceship, and *teach* them how it works. Teach them how to manipulate gravity. Teach them how Faster-Than-Light travel works. Teach them *something*."

G'brael's face wasn't as red now, but he is still controlling the volume of his voice. "This is a very old argument, L'lith," he says. "I've already given them the clues they need to solve those puzzles and others. Emotional motivations might help in the short run, but they can do serious damage in the long run. I've seen it myself."

L'lith pretends to ponder. "Hmm," she says, brushing her chin with the back of her hand. "And since women are more emotionally motivated than men..." After pausing for a few moments she suddenly asks, "Is that why you don't let women vote in Atlantis?"

G'brael is immediately enraged. "That's a bold-faced lie, L'lith! All of our women have the right to vote and some do it, some women even hold office, but many *choose* not to participate."

"Jim Crow Laws," she says under her breath. "Let me guess," she counters. "Some actions reduce estrogen and politics is one of them."

He nods and says, "No... it increases *testosterone*. The aggression and competition needed increases *testosterone* in women. "Both genders make both hormones, but estrogen is significantly greater in women while testosterone is significantly greater in men. A woman's behavior reduces the *ratio* of estrogen to testosterone and makes them more masculine."

She balks. "Women don't *have* testosterone," she tells him.

Exasperated, he sighs. "Then why do women take 'hormone replacement pills' after menopause?" he asks. "People make many different choices for many different reasons, not the same choice for the same reason. Voting is a choice... not a mandate. People are individuals, not cattle."

She looks at him for a moment. "Moo," she mimics. "Clever rationalization, G'brael," she tells him. "You're not going to help the Americans. Are you?"

"We already did," he says. "We took away their road-blocks and gave them the clues they need to solve everything for themselves."

L'lith looks at the ground and shakes her head. "It's a real tragedy when parents refuse to be parents," she says. Then announcing to the room again, "The Osirian people will help you. We'll teach you about gravity, Faster-Than-Light technology and even alien life."

Excitement fills the room like oxygen, filling every person with desire. Many cheer and others chant, "Osiria! Osiria! Osiria!"

An enormous man, at least seven feet tall, enters the room. Heavily muscled, he wears black battle armor and a cape that reaches the floor. It has the same black overside with blue underside colors as L'lith's cape. He has short-cropped hair and a pointed goatee. Gasping at the sight of him, the people fall silent. "P'al!" G'brael says, astonished.

"*General* P'al," L'lith corrects him. "You have your First, Harwell has his and so do I." She turns to Harwell, "This is General P'al, Supreme Commander of the Cherubim." General Hamilton notices the six silver stars on his collar: Five in the shape of a pentagon and one in the middle.

G'brael calmly whispers to President Harwell, "The Osirian army."

L'lith is annoyed and says, "G'brael, shouldn't you be leaving?"

G'brael fakes a smile. "Time to go, S'lon," he says loudly, then whispers to President Harwell, "This will be the greatest test Mankind has ever known. Choose wisely." G'brael starts to walk out the door. "I know you will," he says, patting the president on the shoulder again. Having lost the crowd at the eleventh hour, G'brael and S'lon can do nothing more than to silently walk out of the room.

The Ancient Greek sophist Flavius Philostratus wrote of three types of dragons infesting ancient India. Many of his reports sound like 'men' operating machines. It emits a fire brighter than any torch, a burrowing dragon sounds like clashing brass, there are colorful gems in a dragon's head and so on. Other parts of his reports do not. Dragons enjoy swimming and their heart, liver and meat are all edible. He never mentions breathing fire or flying, but noted that the Greek poet Homer described them better than other poets. More descriptions? Lost knowledge? Is this a living creature operating machinery?

Chapter 7

There Be Dragons!

Dr. Livingston is hovering over his computer screen when Richard walks into the office. "Richard, you won't *believe* the data the satellites got today. It's amazing! Staggering stuff!"

Richard calmly stands in front of Bill's desk, "Bill, you didn't see the news. Did you?"

Bill spares a moment's glance at Richard before looking back to his precious computer screen. "I don't watch TV very often. It's all about bad, worse and even worse. By the way, here's the ten bucks I owe you." Already having it handy, he slaps two five-dollar bills onto the desk without looking up. "You were right. They were like a pack of wolves, ready to attack. They were only interested in making it sound like a disaster, *then* they brought up the dinosaurs and California."

Ignoring the money, Richard sighs and calmly sits on the corner of Bill's desk. "Well, I have a feeling they'll be banging on your door before the day is out."

Bill stops and looks at where Richard sat, then looks at his face. "Richard, this stuff is amazing, yes, but it still has to be verified by several sources. It'll take some time. By the end of the *week*, maybe, but…"

Richard jumps off the desk. "BILL, aliens landed on the White House lawn this morning!"

Stunned, as if waking up from a dream, "What?" he says.

Richard yells again, *"Close Encounters, E.T., They're here!* It all went down this morning!"

Bill looks amused. "That was *Poltergeist*," he says. "Ghosts, not aliens." Bill sits back in his chair and without batting an eyelash, he says, "You know I've thought about that. Personally I think there are several species of aliens."

"We know that, too, Bill," he says.

Bill sits forward in his chair. "You saw the dragons?"

Richard is stunned for a moment and looks at him blankly. "I didn't see any dragons, Bill," he says, "but there were humans and a couple of gray alien-things."

Bill immediately closes the files on his computer screen and opens new ones. Here is the ancient Greek word for *dragon* and here's the one for *serpent*." Richard walks around the desk and looks at the screen. "They aren't spelled alike," he says, "but they *sound* similar. Remember that most people at this time would be illiterate. Dragons are reptiles that fly in Europe, walk in Asia and only breathe fire sometimes. A snake slithers. They knew that. They weren't talking about snakes. That's a totally different word. Bill opens file after file on his computer. "Finnish, Norse, Celtic, Germanic, Polish, French and Macedonian legends all talk about flying, fire-breathing dragons. Some even have historical accounts." Richard doubted everything so far, but he knew better than to interrupt Bill when he got going with something! "Mayan, Aztec, Egyptian, Sumerian, Persian, Chinese, Japanese and Korean legends talk of flying serpent that did *not* breathe fire. Christian, Chinese, Korean, Jewish and Islamic mythologies talk of a reptile, usually calling it a serpent, which would *walk* and even *speak*. I can go on and on. I think all these cultures were talking about the *same thing*."

Richard stops him. "Wait a minute, Bill!" he says. "How are these anything like each other?" "Humans are hard-wired to think of reptiles as dangerous creatures. It's probably something leftover from evolution." Richard sometimes unconsciously gives Bill hints about his true intelligence.

Bill smiles for a moment. "A sentient reptile in a fighter jet," he says confidently.

Richard bursts out laughing. "Oh, come on, Bill!" he manages. "You've gone off the deep end on this one! Ooh!" he says, waving his hands around. He pretends to whisper a secret. "I heard that Bigfoot is behind a lot of this stuff. He's an *alien*."

Bill just rolls his eyes and quietly takes the ridicule. He's used to it. After a few minutes, Richard runs out of jokes and Bill starts to work on him. "Think of it scientifically," he says.

Richard stops laughing and listens, but maintains his smirk. "Okay," he says.

"All these cultures have dragon legends," Bill starts. "One possible explanation is an evolutionary fear of reptiles. Some cultures emphasize that fear more than others."

Richard nods. "That's right," he says.

Bill continues, "I suggest that dragons are an intelligent species of reptiles in fighter jets." Richard snickers, but manages not to say anything. A creature with wings is just a metaphor for a creature that *can* fly, either naturally or mechanically. The word *serpent* is another word for *reptile*. Something that 'breathes fire' is yet another metaphor for 'cause fire from a distance.' Richard stops snickering and stares intently at Bill's computer screen. "Hindu mythology talks about Garuda, a bird-like creature, the mount of the god Vishnu and sworn enemy of the Naga serpent race. Polish records mention the *olophagus* Smok. They don't call it a dragon. Other people do. You know what *olophagus* means. Don't you?"

Richard swallows and closes his eyes. "Swallows whole," he says quietly.

"A bird and reptile trait," he says, beaming with delight. "'Homer's City of Troy' was thought to be a story... until Heinrich Schliemann uncovered it in 1868. Homer intuitively described the feet of male versus female crayfish and later described the red back of a marsh dragon. People even say Grendel was a walking dragon."

Richard opens his eyes and asks, "From *Beowulf*?"

"Yep," Bill excitedly answers. "Grendel can rip men apart to swallow them, and even a razor-sharp sword can't penetrate his skin. Sound familiar? Beowulf grabbed Grendel by the hand... and you know the rest. I always wondered why Beowulf could grab Grendel by the hand and not have his own arm ripped off. He can rip a man apart, but his arms can't do it."

Richard is genuinely interested now. "So if he doesn't use his hands, then how does he rip the man apart?" Bill grabs an apple off his desk, sinks his teeth into it and then turns his head to rip a chunk out of it. "I see!" Richard says.

"You know," Bill starts, "*T. rex's* arms were tiny compared to his body, but they were only slightly larger than human arms. In an arm-wrestling match, the *T. rex* has the strength to win, but couldn't rotate his arm enough to finish the match. The story says that Grendel pulled his arm too close, and Beowulf used a sword to cut off the arm. Beowulf doesn't have enormous strength. He has a deep understanding of skeletal structure... and experience."

Richard scoffs, "Eighth century England is nowhere near the Cretaceous Period!"

Bill calmly replies, "Not a *Tyrannosaurus Rex*, but something with a similar skeleton. A reptile with a bird's skeleton, a Theropod. Believe it or not, *T.* rex was the 4th smartest of *all* the dinosaurs."

Richard gasps. "You kidding me? Right?" he asks, looking for a glimmer of humor in his eyes. Bill wasn't joking. "I've always thought of him as a big, dumb brute!" he says.

Bill retorts. "Brute, yes. Dumb, no." Bill laughs to himself. "At least in the world of *dinosaurs*, he was smart. Most dinosaurs were just big, dumb lizards... but things were changing. *All* of the top 10 smartest dinosaurs were Theropods! Paleontologists look at the imprint of their brain on the inside of their skull."

Richard shakes his head, again. "I don't know," he says. "I'm with you on the dinosaurs, but your theory sounds flimsy to me, but I *also* know your theories have a habit of coming true."

As if trying to prove his theory again, "I have more than that," he says. "Much more."

"It's okay, Bill," he says. "I know better than to doubt you."

Bill looks relieved. "Going back to our original conversation," he says, "at this thing at the White House with the aliens. Were there any misshapen humans?"

Richards looks at Bill and says, "Now that you mention it, there was one guy that was really, really tall and muscular. He also talked funny."

Bill points with his finger. "That's him," he says. "That's the dragon. He's in disguise." Bill sinks into his chair and scratches his chin, "Hmmm," he says. "The gray aliens weren't in disguise, but he was. I wonder what he's up to?"

Later That Night

Alone is his office, Dr. Livingston marks on a world map that lay on the table behind his computer chair. A picture of L'lith and General P'al lay next to drawings of dragons and the accounts of dragons by ancient witnesses. He continues to replay the digital broadcast of L'lith's comments about the underwater cities. Over the years, he has found that saying his thoughts out loud helps him to generate new ideas. "Most of the underwater cities lay on the Northern and the Southern 30° latitudes", he says to himself. "I wonder why."

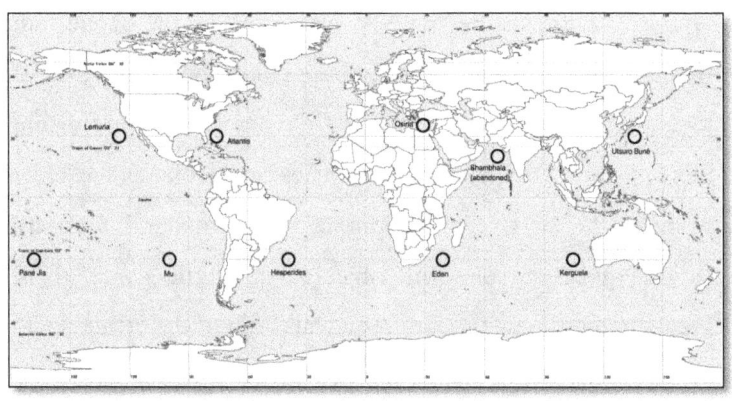

The computer voice alerts him. "Your data has finished compiling," it announces.

He whirls his chair around. "Oh! Good!" he says. "I remember having seen ozone signatures on these graphs before," he mutters as he opens a colorful, 3-D graph of radio frequencies recorded. There's a *lot*. "but it didn't occur to me that this was proof of alien life," he says, finishing his thought. "Well... plant life," he adds.

Dr. Livingston frowns. "I can see that the radio frequencies for ozone are here, and I can tell the computer which ones to select, but it's all lumped together. I can't tell from which areas of the sky that these radio frequecies are coming." Thoughtful for a moment, he suddenly sits up in his chair, opens a new computer window and starts feverishly typing. "This will be fun," he says. "Make the ozone radio frequencies to display in a sky blue color, then route the data to the university's planetarium." He types a bit more, finishing the transfer. He stands up, stretches and looks at the clock. "Whoa!" he says. "It's midnight! No wonder I feel stiff! Well, I guess no one will object to my little game, then!" Lazily gathering a few things, he walks out of the office door.

As expected, the planetarium is completely deserted. It is a medium-sized, round room with several rows of auditorium-style folding seats arranged in a big circle. Almost everything is black, except the white, half-dome-shaped ceiling above him. It's like being inside a globe! Dr. Livingston types a few commands on the planetarium computer's keyboard and the room lights suddenly dim, showing a remarkably realistic representation of twilight. Stars begin to appear on the sunken, round ceiling as the scene progresses into night. "Okay", he says as he leans over and types on the keyboard again. He looks up, looks back at the computer screen, then looks up again while squinting. "The data I sent is displaying up there, but I can't see *any* difference. Let me try this." He types a few more commands and stars fade away, leaving several points of blue on the ceiling. "Oh my God!" he gasps. "It was here the whole time and I never saw it! This is proof... *solid proof* of alien life." He stands there, daydreaming about the Nobel Prize he *could* have won, then snaps back to reality. He frowns, "Alien *plant* life, that is."

Livingston stares at the blue dots on the ceiling for a few minutes. "Naturally-occurring oxygen isn't breathable, but plants use photosynthesis to convert carbon dioxide into sugars while converting water into breathable oxygen. So where there is ozone, there is breathable oxygen. Where there is breathable oxygen, there are aliens plants. Where there are alien plants, there *might be* alien animals or even something higher." He unconsciously walks to one of the theater chairs, and as he starts to sit down, jumps up and darts over to the computer again. "This is the sky in Earth's *Northern* Hemisphere," he mutters. The blue dots on the ceiling move, almost as though someone is spinning a huge globe. "They are going to attack a planet in the Reticulum constellation, and that's in Earth's *Southern* Hemisphere." He turns on the Constellation Identifier to help him, and quickly finds the correct constellation, nearly in the center of the sky. There is a blue dot outside the Reticulum constellation itself, near the Horologium constellation. "Hmm," he mumbles. He types on the computer's keyboard again and the blue dot quickly enlarges to be a couple of feet across, with a white star right next it. "Zeta-2 Reticuli," he announces under his breath. He cocks his head back. "I've heard of that star."

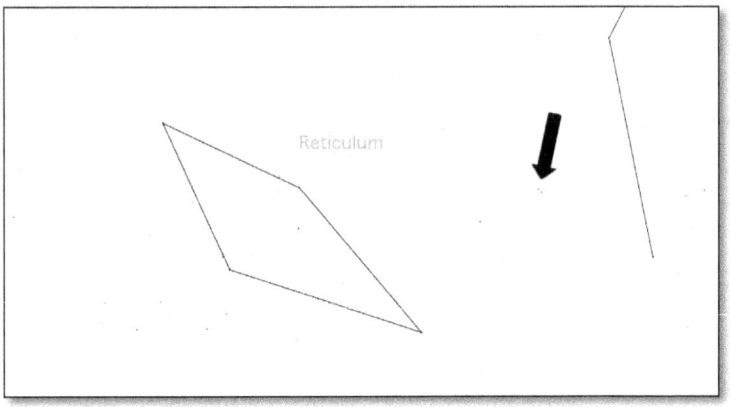

The sudden wealth of the Knights Templar is no mystery at all. In the middle of the 12th century, Pope Innocent II issued a papal bull, endorsing the Knights Templar and freeing them from any taxation. Taxes act like compound interest against individuals, so the smaller the better. The Knights Templar decided to become bankers, compounding their money further. The biggest buildings in any city are usually banks. By making profit and not paying taxes, they amassed enormous wealth. Less than two centuries later, another pope helped to hunt them down.

Chapter 8

The Nine Underwater Cities

Harwell sits down with his new Osirian friends in the same conference room. Asher and several others are still with them. In the interest of popular support, the White House is still broadcasting the meetings all around the world. Thinking of glistening underwater cities of light, Harwell offers L'lith a cup of coffee and says, "Tell us what Osiria looks like."

She smiles. "Osiria would look a lot like Manhattan, if you turned it upside-down and each building were two hundred stories," L'lith explains. She brushes her chin with the back of her hand. "Of course, it's much larger than Manhattan... and not so spread-out. There are hundreds of buildings, all arranged in a thirty-mile-wide circle. One hundred million people live there."

Harwell nearly spits out his coffee. "One hundred *million*?!" he asked in astonishment. "Our entire country is that big!" General Hamilton shoots a look at Asher. "Why haven't our submarines seen it, yet?" he asks. "Surely they saw all the lights." The general shoots Asher another look.

L'lith laughs. "The lights are on the inside, not the outside," she says. The buildings look like a cross between a skyscraper and a bunker. The buildings are wide, angular and very deep. Since they are underground, you probably wouldn't notice them even if you used ground-penetrating sonar. They'd probably look like pieces of bedrock. "All ten cities use or used, the same idea: Many very tall buildings, buried deep in the ocean floor. There are nine other cities like Osiria, seven of which are human."

Harwell's freezes with his eyes open wide, like a deer caught in the headlights. "There are aliens living on Earth?" he asks. Asher keeps his mouth shut.

L'lith doesn't bat an eyelash. "Yes and no," she says. "The Lemurians live in two cities, and Foreign Nationals visit all the time." Harwell makes no secret of his apprehension. "You must keep in mind," she says, "that Lemurians evolved on Earth three hundred million years before humans even arrived. They'd 'met their neighbors' a long time ago."

Harwell slowly and timidly puts down his cup. "From *our* point of view, this is all very sudden," he says quietly. He clears his throat. "Tell me more about these cities. Where are they, and what are they called?"

She thinks for a moment and continues. "Pané Jia is east of New Zealand, Mu is west of Chile, Hesperides lies east of Paraguay, Eden is southeast of Africa and Kerguela lies west of Australia. Atlantis is just east of your state of Florida, Lemuria is just west of your state of California, Utsuro Buné is near Japan, Shambhala was abandoned and lies near India and Osiria is east of Cypress in the Mediterranean." She takes a sip of the coffee. "Mmm," she says. "I have something like this on my ship. It's very relaxing. Mu and Lemuria are Lemurian cities. Osiria was a blessing in disguise."

"Oh?" Harwell asks. "How is that?" he asks.

"Osiria was an island nation and a rival of Atlantis," he began. "It... had an accident... and was destroyed. The people of Osiria were rescued at the same time as the Atlanteans. They eventually built an underwater city near the island and called it Atlantis, also. No underwater cities would exist if it weren't the Osirian's harnessing of volcanic energy."

Several moments go by until Harwell breaks the silence. "I'm sorry," he tells her, "but this alien thing is affecting me. I mean, we've found planets out there but nothing alive."

L'lith looks around. "Don't tell G'brael I said this," she begins then loudly whispers, "but his people are exquisite engineers." Back to her full voice again, "The spaceships of the past were shoddy and barely functional - virtual deathtraps that crashed all the time. They used spinning mercury, ion wind, magnets, gyroscopes, air pressure suspension and even rockets and airfoils. All of these inventions had been in alien possession for millions of years, but it's like they stumbled onto those things one day. They can mentally calculate and remember exquisitely but are complete *idiots* about everything else. You have to see it to understand it. They've accumulated some wonderful technologies but only because of the enormous amounts of time involved. G'brael's people changed all that – *true* anti-gravity, a sleek design, air and marine capability, simple operation and the use of minuscule amounts of power. It's like having the performance of a Ferrari with the simplicity of a video game. In the last 20 or

30 years they came up with true mental controls. You don't even need to be a pilot. Just think it, and the ship will do it. Most races buy from them. Of course, somehow, some of these *idiot* aliens manage to crash one every now and then." She pretends to whisper a secret again. "Can you tell I don't like them?" she asks.

"Anyway," she says. "I think his people's success has made G'brael arrogant. He says that even government should be mathematically designed. He's living in a dream world! A good leader *takes* power! People are like small children. They need to be *told* what to do. If they don't do it, then spank them and spank them hard. Certain people understand this better than others. An even smaller number of people have the stomach for spanking spoiled brats."

She takes another sip of her drink and completely changes the subject. "All intelligent species breathe oxygen," she tells him. "It takes breathable oxygen to make collagen and collagen glues multiple cells together. It reacts strongly while fairly stable and it…"

Asher breaks-in, "Why collagen? Why not something else? It *is* an alien planet."

"Some things, Mr. Asher," she says, "are universal: Collagen, chlorophyll, cells, ozone, breathable oxygen.

Another basic thing is that breathable oxygen makes ozone. That's how we find Earth-like planets." She starts to sip her drink again, but finishes talking first. "I won't bore you with the details, but we simply look at the reflective spectrum of ozone... in the radio range, of course." She takes another sip of the coffee.

Asher can't sit still. He stands up and blurts out, "Ozone! That is brilliant!" Turning to Harwell he says, "Mr. President, stars can't make ozone! There'd be no interference from the star at all!"

Harwell leans back in his chair, "Don't we already do stuff like that?" he asks.

Asher is in his element. "Sort of, Sir, but not really. We map the sky with radio telescopes, we listen for signals and we sometimes look at the composition of stars but not like this. We have probably seen it and glossed right over it. We've focused on 'the wobble effect' and stars 'dimming' when a planet gets in front of it, but none are Earth-like. They're all giant planets. None have breathable air, water or safe temperatures."

L'lith translates for him. "None have life," she tells him.

Asher turns from L'lith back to Harwell, "Yes! Yes! Ozone is made from breathable oxygen and only *plants* can make breathable oxygen!" Asher is ready to jump out of his chair. "Receiving those radio frequencies is absolute and positive proof of alien life!"

L'lith puts her cup on the table. "I didn't realize you are so interested in alien life," she announces innocently. "Did G'brael tell you about the Reticulans?" Harwell shrugs his shoulders while looking around.

Asher translates again, "The Grays, Mr. President."

Harwell points to the door and says, "Oh! They were here earlier."

"No, Mr. President," Asher says. He breathes quietly to summon patience. "Those were the Lemurians." Then turning to L'lith, "He never told us about the Reticulans."

"Well," she tells them, "they'll be your first problem. They won't like it if you simply leave this star system."

Harwell looks at her. "What do they care?" he asks.

L'lith picks up her cup and saucer, but does not raise them to her mouth. "The Lemurians and the Grays fought an enormous war many millions of years ago. The Lemurians tried using a new weapon using the heat from inside the Earth. The plan backfired, melting a huge area of the Earth's crust and causing a mass extinction of Earth's animals. The Grays used the situation to their advantage by firing mass drivers. By the way, that's why you have uranium on the surface of Earth. I'm surprised that humans didn't notice that something *that* heavy didn't sink into the Earth a long time ago. It's like seeing a brick floating on water and *not* thinking, 'Why?'. The Lemurians escaped by building homes underwater."

Asher rubs his chin with his fingers. "I've always wondered about that," he says to himself.

L'lith lifts her cup to drink, but talks instead. "The Grays banned any inhabitant of Earth from leaving this star system. Since that time, the Grays have developed robots that look *exactly* like themselves. Did G'brael tell you about S'lon?" She takes a quick sip of her drink.

Harwell looks at Asher. Understanding the look, he says, "Yes. A perfect android."

"Yes and no," she says. "The biological Grays made too many of these robots, were over-run and were destroyed millions of years ago. Computers are notoriously literal. The biological Grays meant the Lemurians, but with the biological Grays gone there was no one to interpret an imperfectly written restriction for the android Grays."

Asher looks heart-broken. "Humans can't leave, either. Can we?"

"Just this star system," she confirms. "But Mars and Venus are fair game," she says. "Both are great terraforming projects! There was no need for us to do it, but we've thought about this for you to do... with our help, of course. Mars is an easier project, but it's still a really big project. Just put a lot of heavy material on over Mars. Asteroid iron will work nicely. We can just drop several of the bigger asteroids on the surface. That'll stretch the fabric of space and make the planet much heavier. Increased gravity will pull the atmosphere together and warm the air." She laughs to herself, "Of course, there's not much air or warmth to begin with," she comments. "Increased gravity will also increase pressure in the planet's core, warming it up and letting it generate a magnetic field. Then hit it with a few hundred water-ice asteroids and a few hundred nitrogen-ice asteroids. Let it sort itself out for a little while and you'll have a new planet!"

General P'al speaks for the first time. L'lith turns her head to look at him. "It will need a large moon," he says with his ultra-deep voice.

She pauses for a moment, looking at him, then talks to the people in the room again. "Yes," she says. "G'brael's people tried to use two moons for stability. It needs much less 'moon,' but it has to work precisely. It works great on paper, but no so well in practice. You can construct a large moon out of asteroid iron and Stannum or simply drag another moon over to it. Triton is a good candidate. It'd be a good nitrogen source."

General Hamilton shakes his head, "What you're talking about sounds nice and everything, but it's *preposterous*! We sometimes have trouble just getting into space; much less moving moons like they were marbles! If we were gods..."

L'lith cuts him off. "We *are* the gods," she says flatly. The room seems to echo with her words. The general stops dead in his tracks. "And yes, we *can* move moons like they were marbles. All of this is because of our technology... which we are giving to you. That makes *you* gods, too."

General Hamilton looks stunned and stands there with his mouth partly open. He starts to say something then stops. He seems to think of something else, starts to say it and then stops again. Finally he utters the word, "Okay," and steps back a little.

A dull silence fills the room for about the millionth time today. Asher breaks it. "If we are gods now, then why are we stuck here on Earth?"

"You have more problems more immediate than the Grays," she warns.

Harwell must have dozed off though part of the conversation because he woke up saying, "What?"

L'lith answers him. "When the Earth crosses the galactic plane. Today. It will put pressure on Earth's planet core. Normally it's not a problem, but human activity has changed that. This time, pressure will relieve itself in a super-volcanic eruption... Yellowstone Park. With all of that happening at one time, the magnetic field will move. Sedona, Arizona, will be your new north pole... the *magnetic* north pole, that is. Water is weakly diamagnetic, and will follow the magnetic field. The Gulf of Mexico will split your county in two by completely flooding many of your states. Japan will be completely submerged and the Mediterranean Sea will nearly drain. That doesn't even include the acid rain or the ash cloud from the super-volcano."

Harwell decides to comment, "Maybe the ash cloud is a good thing. It can cool down our Global Warming situation."

L'lith shoots a menacing look at him. "It'll cool you down. Very well. It'll block out much of the sun and it's warmth for nearly two years. There's be acid rain, crops will fail without the sunlight, starvation will follow and then people will start freezing to death in the summer. But at least the planet will be cooler. All religions lie! Including the religion of Global Warming or whatever you're calling it this week!"

"Climate change," Asher tells her in a quiet voice.

"Weather!" she bellows. "That figures!"

Harwell tries to retract his comment, "I'm sorry. I…"

L'lith cuts him off, suddenly much calmer. "It wasn't you, Harwell. It was me." She speaks with a stoic voice and her eyes glisten with tears, but none fall. "As much as I know and as much as I see, I can't do anything about it. This isn't *my* planet. It's yours. You aren't *my* people, you're G'brael's people. All I can do is protect the survivors." She looks at Asher. "Do you see how your problems are more immediate than the Grays?" Asher nods and she turns her attention back to Harwell. "We can take some of your people underwater with us and we can relocate some of them deep underground on Mars. That'll keep them out of harm's way while it's being terraformed. But I'm afraid that we can't accommodate *all* of your people. Our underwater city is only designed for 100 million people and we have people of our own. A lot of people will just have to stay here." She hangs her head. "I'm sorry to say that some of your people will survive, and some won't."

One of the aids thinks out loud. "It'll be like Hurricane Katrina all over again," he says.

L'lith continues, "Unfortunately it will be... a *planetary* Hurricane Katrina. We have ships that can take all of you, but there's no *place* to take you. Until we dig underground homes for all of you, Mars is too dangerous. The Hephaes work fast; 24 hours a day and 7 days a week, but it'll take them a decade to build 7 billion underground homes. You don't have that long."

Harwell ventures the question, "What is that?"

"THOSE," she says, a fleeting flare of anger visible. She quickly calms herself with a quick breath. "Are construction robots," she answers. Continuing her thought, "If we didn't have to build underground homes for you, we'd be able to save more of you. Maybe even all of you."

Harwell ventures another question. "Mr. Asher is right. What is the point in being gods if we're stuck here on Earth?"

L'lith smiles, as if waiting for *him* to ask that question. "We don't have much time so I'm going to tell you... in private... from leader to leader," she says.

He assures her, "Everyone here can be trusted."

She keeps her mouth closed and points to the broadcast equipment, lowers her head and touches two fingers to her temple.

The room, the people, everything vanishes in an instant. Harwell finds himself walking with L'lith in the White House's Rose Garden. Snow covers the ground, the walkways are perfectly clear and the sun gleams in the wintery sky. He doesn't realize there has been a transition. Everything seems perfectly natural. L'lith is still wearing her dress and armor while he wears a trench coat. Blowing lightly, the wind carries the smell of snowy air. "Are you cold?" he asks.

She answers him without emotion. "I'm not concerned about the weather," she says. "The situation with the Grays is more serious than I mentioned earlier. Ears were listening at the time."

"I understand," he says.

L'lith clasps her hands together, nervously rolling her hands. "They're coming for you... all of you."

Harwell feels like his heart just fell into his stomach. He stops walking. "Wh... What do you mean?"

L'lith swallows, "G'brael put you in danger, but the danger was coming anyway. This way gives you a fighting chance."

Harwell tries to gulp, but his mouth is too dry. "Danger?" he horsely whispers.

She nods. "The Grays have two criteria for destroying a people: A means of destroying them, and a way of *getting* to them."

Harwell starts to say something, but she cuts him off. "Intent doesn't matter," she tells him. "We're talking about robots. Remember?" She obviously answered his question because he stays quiet and listens. "Your people became targets when your people created nuclear weapons." Harwell starts to say something again, but she cuts him off again. "They're robots! They don't *have* a pity gene!" Harwell closes his mouth again. "Now that you have a means of destroying them *and* a way of getting to them, your time is almost up. They will attack... now."

Rubbing his face with one hand, "G'brael told me that this will be the greatest test that Mankind has ever faced," he says.

Agitated, L'lith tightens her lips, takes a deep breath, then says, "He wasn't kidding. Was he?"

Harwell sighs deeply. Still cupping part of his face, "No, he wasn't," he replies.

"I tried to buy time by telling you how to terraform Mars," she says, "But I doubt it'll work in time."

Harwell sighs again. "How long do you think we have?" he asks.

L'lith looks at the pavement. "We're talking about machines," she says. "They don't sleep, there's no 'proper chain of command,' there's no paperwork to file and *certainly* no laziness." She sighs. "If they were biological I'd say two or three weeks, but with robots it'll be more like a two or three *days*. Maybe sooner."

Harwell sighs loudly, yet again. "I really need General Hamilton here to help me make military decisions."

They start walking again. "Why?" she asks. "You're a perfectly capable man," she pushes. "You don't need such a violent... man... making military decisions for you."

While trying not to offend his new benefactor, Harwell defends his friend, "Alan Hamilton is not a violent man. He takes my ideas and turns them into something the troops can understand."

L'lith nods her head. "So you're saying that he simply regurgitates your orders then acts like he did you a favor." Harwell looks at her, thinks for a few moments and then nods. "I think he's a soulless creature that should be getting coffee for you," she tells him. "An evolved monkey like him doesn't deserve such a high-ranking position. Why don't you tell *me* your ideas?" she asks. "I know our starships and their abilities better than he would anyway."

Harwell hesitates for a split second, then blurts out his thoughts to her. "I think we need to hit them first," he says. "Maybe if we hit them a little bit, they'll just leave us alone."

L'lith shakes her head. "No. You need to hit them so hard that they can't get up again - then kick them some more," she says, kicking her foot.

Harwell looks disturbed. "But those people!" he exclaims.

Mustering patience with a quick breath, "They are *not* people," she tells him. "They are robots. Machines... run amuck. And even if they *were* people," she pleas, "they're trying to kill us... all of us. America isn't the only one in danger here, but only America has the skills to pull this off. That's why we came here. This isn't just a National Security issue," she tells him, "this is *Planetary* Security issue. Americans and non-Americans alike will suffer the consequences if your people don't take action. Harwell looks at her face, but still seems disturbed by the plan. She changes her tactic. "We can do something else, if you'd prefer," she says. "We'll destroy their ships so they can't get to us and then their factories so they can't build more ships." She smiles.

Harwell smiles as well. "I like the second plan better," he tells her. "That would save hundreds or even thousands of lives." L'lith doesn't say anything. He thinks for a minute. "Okay," he says. "Let's do it!"

L'lith smiles. "I think that will be a very popular idea," she tells him. Getting down to business, "How many nuclear missiles do you have?"

He begins to answer, "Actually," then realizes what she asked. "What?!" he exclaims.

She explains, "If you detonate a nuclear missile high in the atmosphere, it creates an EMP, Electro-Magnetic Pulse. Any circuitry that isn't shielded well enough will become useless. Spaceships, weapons and communications will all become paperweights. That'll tremendously reduce casualties. We'll use a *lot* of missiles and take out their entire operation." Partly talking to herself, "It doesn't matter how many you have," she says. "We'll just ride in on our huge spaceships and simply take them from other countries. This *is* Planetary Security. They all have to contribute."

Deeply conflicted, Harwell wrestles with the idea. "We should ask first and let them volunteer the missiles."

L'lith sneers at the idea, "You can always count on people to do the wrong thing. Take them and be done with it!"

Harwell seems to struggle with the idea for a few moments before accepting it. "We'll put your people in Osirian ships to launch a massive pre-emptive strike. To make the strike big enough, we'll use every nuclear weapon on this planet," she says, recapping and expanding the plan. "In case their equipment is shielded, we'll just land a few of those punches. That will rid you and the rest of the galaxy, of the oppressive Gray Empire once and for all," she says with triumphant glee. "That'll have the added effect," she says, "of leveling the playing field here on Earth. No one on this planet will have nuclear weapons."

Any conflict Harwell felt was gone now. "I feel better already," he says.

L'lith stops and turns to face him, "You shouldn't let people tell you what to do."

His face drops. "I know," he says. "People make fun of me and think I don't understand."

"But they're wrong. Aren't they?" she says. "You're smarter than people give you credit."

Harwell nods. "My old boss underestimated me," he tells her. His blue eyes meet her green ones. "I certainly showed him. I'm President now!"

She starts walking again. "And making military decisions *completely* on your own," she says. "It feels good. Powerful. Doesn't it?

He walks with her. "Yes, it does," he says. "I feel like a kid who took his mother's car and got away with it."

L'lith looks at him. "America has already achieved global dominance," she tells him, "and now it has the opportunity for *galactic* dominance." She looks at him. "It just needs a strong and forceful leader to make it happen," she says. "Can you be forceful?"

Harwell puffs out his chest a bit. "They won't know what hit them. Any of them," he says. L'lith smiles and touches two fingers to her temple again.

A country that splits into two countries will scuffle with the other side and escalate into a war. Eventually the 'more aggressive' side will overtake the other. It's a cycle. Oaths of allegiance, personal ridicule, second-class citizenship and financial turmoil will go on and on for several generations. Secession is just not worth the price. But a country that splits into three, five or seven new countries (an odd number) can prevent such an agonizing cycle.

Chapter 9

Preparing For War

Harwell conducts a debriefing without General Hamilton. "Ansibles will give us real-time reconnaissance from modified comets," Harwell tells a small group of high-ranking military officers. He stands near a large screen, pointing at it and explaining his plan. "A team will go to the Gray's star system and install dozens of sensors and receivers into natural comets, while it is still near the outer planets. They will record everything. Normally that would help us plan the attack, but this is not a normal situation."

One of the lowest-ranking officers there, a Colonel, says, "With respect, Mr. President, you're talking about updates and not reconnaissance. It would take months or years for this to help us."

A two-star general asks, "Mr. President, why isn't this a normal situation? Success comes from good intelligence and a lot of planning."

Harwell ignores the Colonel, briefly looking at the CIA Director who had been lurking in the corner. "Already done," he says, answering the Two Star. "These are sensors of Osirian design. It won't take months."

The Colonel nervously swallows before offering advice. "Mr. President, sensors can be placed on natural comets as you said. They can then help identify military targets and avoid civilians. A single nuclear weapon exploded several miles above each target will cripple their defenses with EMPs…"

Harwell cuts him off, "I've heard that plan, Colonel. It's too slow, and I think it's for wimps." Harwell raises his voice, "This is the BIG ONE people! The survival of the human race and every other race out there, is in our hands… right now! Others have tried half-assed attacks like that! They're dead now! All of them!" Harwell stops, takes a breath and speaks to them again. "The enemy is deceptive and cunning," he tells them, using his *Inside Voice*. "Military-looking targets are actually decoys while civilian-looking houses launch starfighters. These are robots, not flesh and blood creatures. There are no civilians and there are no *true* casualties. Nothing can be off-limits. Surprise..." he tells the entire group. "Surprise will be our greatest weapon. The modified comets will help us to identify targets. Military bases with ships must be destroyed. We don't want them able to hit back. I want to hit them with a sledgehammer! Then hit them again and again!"

General Harwell hurriedly walks in the room. "I apologize, Mr. President. I wasn't informed about this meeting"

Harwell walks over to him and shakes his hand. "That's quite alright, General. You weren't invited," he says, still clasping his hand and a smile on his face.

General Hamilton starts to laugh but sees the look in Harwell's eyes. He breaks away. "Y... You're serious, aren't you?"

"Aren't you, *Sir*," Harwell corrects him.

The general steps back a little. "Yes, Sir. I'm sorry, Mr. President," he says, choosing his words carefully. "It won't happen again, Sir."

Harwell is still smiling. "You're dismissed, General" he says.

As Harwell starts to turn to leave, General Hamilton speaks up, "Mr. President, you are planning a preemptive nuclear attack on millions of people."

Harwell turns to face the general and closes his eyes. "Robots," he says and then opens his eyes again. "Robots, General. I'm planning to turn millions of machines off. Does that warrant your presence? This mission, and this mission alone, is what it will take to keep these machines from ravaging our country or our planet. Again... you are dismissed."

Harwell turns and walks away. General Hamilton stands there for a few moments with his mouth partly open. He hears Harwell telling the others, "We're going to launch every nuke the Human Race has ever built at their planet. I want that place to be a molten ball of... planet by the time we're done with it!" General Hamilton notices the CIA Director, pauses and finally turns to leave the room.

At Asher's Apartment

Asher goes home: Excited, fearful and *exhausted*. He immediately logs in to a chat room and finds his friends, Joe and Tex.

```
Asher:   President  Harwell  isn't  one  of  us
         anymore.
```

Both guys answer at the same time. Tex is being his usual smart-ass self while Joe is being naïve.

```
Tex:     I didn't know you two were buddies.
Joe:     How so?
```

Asher ignores Tex' comment.

```
Asher:   He's  bought  all  of  that  stuff:   Hook,
         line and sinker.
Asher:   I think something else is going on.
```
Tex tries to be serious, for once.

```
Tex:     Why do you think that?
```

Asher types feverishly.

```
Asher:   It just doesn't feel right.  L'lith is
         hiding something.
Tex:     From what you've said, they showed up
         on  a  special  day,  told  us  about  the
         past  and  predicted  a  future  that's
         PROBABLY right.
Tex:     You're worried because...
```

Asher realizes that he sounds like he's just minutes away from wearing a tin foil hat, like those people on TV.

```
Asher:    It may be a paranoid speculation on my
          part, but the most convincing place to
          put a lie is directly between two
          truths.
```

They reply at the same time.

```
Joe:    I see.
Tex:    Oh? Like what?
```

Asher explains.

```
Asher:    G'brael is like a mentor or a
          professor.
Asher:    He pulls answers out of you, while
          L'lith just gives you the answers and
          tells you to start a war.
```

The two reply at the same time, again.

```
Tex:    That isn't good.

Joe:    That isn't good.
```

Asher pauses then asks.

```
Asher:  Can you two meet me, so we can talk?
```

Tex seems to jump.

```
Tex:    You mean In Real Life??
```

Joe: I'm not sure that's such a good idea.

He asks suspiciously.

Asher: What's the big deal, you guys?

Asher: We've been chatting for two years.

Asher: I doubt there are ANY secrets left.

Tex writes, but Joe doesn't reply.

Tex: Why don't you just talk to us here?

Asher pushes a bit more.

Asher: It's just not the same.
Asher: This has been an enormous day for us
         all. I REALLY don't want to be left
         alone with my thoughts.
Tex: You won't.
Tex: We'll go on and on and on and... until
         you fall asleep on the keyboard.

Asher doesn't mince words.

Asher: I feel overwhelmed and I need you guys
         to level me out.
Asher: I need to see your faces.

There's a pause and Joe finally writes:

Joe: Okay, Asher. Just remember that you
         are our best friend in the world.

Asher: Now you're scaring me.

Tex tries to lessen Asher's anxiety, but can't resist a chance to be a smart-ass.

Tex: It's not that bad. We'll meet at the
         coffee shop on G Street NW and 22nd.
Tex: I'll be wearing a coat.
Asher: Very funny, Tex. It's December.
Asher: Everyone's wearing a coat.
Tex: Okay. Okay. A green coat.
Joe: We'll all look for the green coat.

Women aren't pawns. They have shaped Human Civilization from the beginning, but fewer and fewer are aware of that strength. Voting's strength is minuscule compared with motherhood's strength. Ask any new bride about her mother-in-law's influence. Motherhood decreases as political involvement increases... and Mankind suffers from its absence. A mother shapes her child into exactly what SHE wants and rarely what the father wants. Presidents, kings and emperors all have mothers and The hand that rocks the cradle is the hand that rules the world.

Chapter 10

The Meeting

(That Same Evening)

As Asher walks into the coffee shop, he sees that there aren't many people inside. He looks around for his two friends, but only sees an older man with a black jacket, two young women sitting together and a short-haired blond woman ordering at the counter. *Not here yet,* he thinks as he walks past her and finds a place to sit down. He notes that the blond woman is ordering hot chocolate. *She'll need it,* he thinks again. *It's 15 degrees out there!*

After waiting for a few minutes, he notices that one of the two young women is staring at him. *Was this a girl I knew back in college?* he wonders.

Realizing she's been caught, "Asher?" she asks with a slight drawl.

He tries to be polite. "I'm sorry," he says. "Do I know you?"

"It's me," she tells him. "Tex."

Asher **cannot** be more shocked. "No," he says. "This is a joke. Right? The guys are messing with me." The other girl turns around and he recognizes her immediately. "Joanne? What are you doing..." he starts to ask her. He pauses for a second then understands. "Joe," he says, almost like an accusation.

Joanne nearly jumps out of her chair to embrace him. He holds his hands out, like he's keeping her at bay. She stops. "Two years online?" he starts. "And two years ago. Yes, our date was two years ago and now I find out that you've been *stalking* me for the last two years."

Joanne keeps her distance. "I'm so, so sorry, Asher," she tells him, nearly in tears. Other people take notice of the scene. "What can I do to make it up to you?" she begs.

"Just have sex with him," Tex comments. "Everything will be forgiven by morning." They both glare at her. "What?!" she asks. "It's what guys want, anyway," she sneers, but then realizes something and gasps. "Or is this why you liked him in the first place? Real men have feelings, but rarely show them. These north-easterners have them *and* show them... but this one's different." Only then does Asher notice that Tex is wearing a green coat. "Listen," she says. "She's dated lots of guys and most of them are lying horn-dogs. She said she liked you because you were honest, but you weren't living up to your potential. We went *in cognito* to help you, but it went farther than we intended and we're sorry. That's the honest truth."

Asher thinks for a few moments then sighs in defeat. "I've told things to both of you that are... beyond embarrassing." He hangs his head. "There's a lot more to this than just a gender thing. I am truly, truly embarrassed and truly, truly hurt. I believed in and trusted you. And you deceived me. Both of you."

"We're sorry," Tex says.

"But believe it or not," Joanne adds, "we both think you're really, really sweet."

"Thanks," he absently mutters and then turns around and walks to the door.

Joanne tries to stop him. "What did you want to talk about?" she asks.

Asher stops and turns around and says, "Well, it could be about L'lith's conspiracy or interplanetary war or my ex-girlfriend stalking me or my best friends deceiving me about *more than one thing*. Take your pick." He turns around again to walk out.

Tex returns his sarcasm with a little of her own. "Is that the Little Green Men Conspiracy or Humans in UFOs Conspiracy or Little Gray Robots Conspiracy?"

Annoyed, Asher turns around again. "Not funny," he tells her.

Joanne seizes her chance. "How can we help? What can we do?"

"Besides sex," Tex injects. They both glare at her again. She holds her hands up. "Sorry. Sorry. It just comes out sometimes."

That's definitely the Tex I know, he thinks. "I'm really tired," he tells them. "It's going to be insanely busy at work tomorrow and I need to rest. I'll talk to you guys in a few days." Without waiting, he turns and walks out of the shop.

Tex turns to Joanne. "He'll get over it," she says. "And if he doesn't, you can still offer him sex."

Outside, Asher walks home. *It's more of the same,* he thinks. The snow makes crunching sounds under his feet. Normally he likes the sound, but right now he doesn't even want to listen. *I'm honest to other people, and they deceive me.* He walks across street walkways without looking. *Maybe I'll get lucky and get hit,* half-kidding himself. The streets are vacant, covered in two inches of fresh snow and there isn't a single tire track in sight. He suddenly stops walking, right in the middle of the street. *Wait!* he thinks. *I sound like such a self-pitying dweeb!* He looks around. *There may be losers in bars, but not everyone who goes to a bar is a loser.* He starts walking in a new direction. *Tex was right, even though he... she... didn't mean to be.* He picks up the pace. *Drown my sorrows in a few drinks, then pick up a chick. Hell! At this point, I'd pay for a girl! I'm a government worker! I've got money!*

Inside The Building

Inside the bar is just like Asher had imagined it: lowered lights, country music, people laughing and a pool table in the corner. Asher gets a beer at the bar, and sits at a table very near the pool table. He nurses his beer, and quietly watches the game: studying the rules, the geometry of the game and the methods for making really good plays.

After a few more beers, two hours of watching and playing the game in his head; Asher feels confident enough to try it himself. Winning one game would give his confidence a boost, but winning numerous games would give his status in the bar a boost! He would become a *magnet* for a lot of its women!

He notices a young woman, probably barely old enough to come inside of a bar, sporadically coming to the pool table, beating one of the rough-looking men, then blending back into the crowd. Asher knows what she is… a pool shark!

Logic tells him to stay away from the young woman, but his hormones tell him otherwise. She has shiny, medium-length brown hair, blue eyes and a gorgeous body…. And her Daisy Duke shorts show off her smooth and slender legs. He watches her beat another unsuspecting man, then swiftly moves in to talk to the young woman, only half a head shorter than himself. "Most of these people aren't old," he tells her, "but it's nice to see someone about my age."

She looks startled. "Oh!" she gasps. "Yeah! Good to see you, too!"

The young pool shark starts to walk away. "Do you want to play?!" he quickly asks.

She turns around, and fakes a smile. "You're new to the bar scene. Aren't ya?" she asks, as her blue eyes size him up.

Asher looks down at his clothes: a knit shirt, fresh blue jeans and tennis shoes. He looks back up at her. "How can you tell?" he playfully asks.

The young woman smiles. "You're nice... and funny," she tells him. "I like that." She brushes a lock of hair behind her ear. "I don't want to take your money," she says, before turning to walk away again.

Asher can tell from her body language that she *does* want to take his money, and is playing a *different kind* of game with him. He turns it around, though. "Then we won't play for money," he tells her. "If I win, you tell me your name."

She turns around. "That's easy," she tells him. "It's Mary. See? You already won!" She turns to leave, yet again.

"No," Asher refuses. "Your *real* name."

The young pool shark turns around again, this time *without* the smile. Walking up to him, "What is your name?" she asks.

He tosses it back into her court. "Play me, and find out…maybe."

Her face loses *all* sense of humor. Picking up a poolstick, she chalks the tip. "Three minutes," she tells him. "I'll know your name in *three* minutes."

Still being coy. "Maybe," he answers, as he walks around the table. "Maybe not."

A humorless *Mary* racks up the balls, then feigns generosity. "I'll even let you go first," she tells him.

Asher chalks the tip of his poolstick. "Thanks," he tells her. He chalks his left hand, then places the cue ball *directly* on the pool table's mark. Conscious of his body's position, he leans over the pool table, and takes aim. He smacks the cue ball dead its center, sending it directly at the collection of balls. It hits the middle of the 1 ball, sending the other balls… about two inches.

Mary starts to laugh, then quickly covers it up with a pretend cough. Asher is embarrassed. "These balls have more mass than I realized," he tells her.

She nods. "Yes," she says, amidst her coughing. "More mass." Getting over her coughing spurt, she says, "Normally, that's a breaking foul." She takes her turn, anyway, striking the cue ball *hard,* and sending the balls all over the tabletop. The solid green-colored ball falls into a corner pocket. "Solids," she announces. *Mary* gleefully slinks around the pool table, aims her poolstick and sinks a solid red-colored ball. "We can stop all this, if you tell me one thing," she says.

Asher shakes his head, pretending to talk to himself. "Three moves into the game, and she wants to quit so she can learn more about me," he toys with her.

Annoyed, she aims for a solid blue-colored ball, shoots, and it bounces off the two rails of the corner pocket; *barely* missing the shot. *Mary* is briefly upset by the mistake, but only briefly. "Your turn," she says.

Asher chalks the tip of his poolstick *again*, and chalks his hand *again*. Leaning over the table, he lines the cue ball up with the 10 ball. Striking it with a lot more force than last time, the 10 ball skates into the corner pocket.

"Nicely done," she announces. "An easy shot, but did well." Asher's not sure if that was a compliment, or an insult. *Mary* points to the 15 ball. "How about that one?" she baits.

He shakes his head. "No," he says, sticking to his plan. "There are too many balls around it." He lines the cue ball up with the 12 ball, and hits it lightly. The slow-moving cue ball grazes the 12 ball on it's left side and drops it in the side pocket. "I've been *carefully* watching you and other pool players for hours," he says, motioning the hand toward her. "This," holding his hand over the table, "This is geometry. I'm good at geometry. This is also physics. I'm good at physics, too. But this is also about half a dozen other subjects that I don't know very well. That's where observation, and experience come in."

Mary gapes at him. "Are you SERIOUS?? Just play!"

Asher has heard *that* before, and doesn't say another word. He turns around, lines up another ball, shoots and sinks the 9 ball. Not hesitating, he walks around the table, lines up again, shoots and sinks the 13 ball. He smiles as he stands up.

Leaning up against a wooden post. "You're pretty lucky," she tells him.

His smile brightens. "Lucky? Maybe," Asher walks around the table, talking like a college professor. "In my... boring... observations, I noticed small inconsistencies from perfect geometry. The tiny imperfections in the rails or in the felt, make this table unique," he says, holding his hand over the table again. "Knowing where those imperfections are located gives me an edge over other players. It's not much, but it's an edge."

Asher is facing the away from the door, but *Mary* can see two women walking into the bar. She smiles, like the cat that ate the canary. "I'm gonna put this bet in high gear," she starts. "If you sink the 8 ball on this *very next* shot, I'll go home with you." Asher grins from ear to ear. "If not," she says, "then you have to leave the bar. Of course!" she adds, "You can still leave with one of *those* two." She points to the two women, who are already getting a lot of attention. "Recognize what they are?" she asks.

He stares at the women, then turns back to *Mary*. "Prostitutes?" he asks in a lowered voice.

She looks at the women. "*Oh* yes," she answers. "There are more hookers in D.C. than Vegas and A.C., combined. They're a lot more discrete here, though."

He leans over the table, then looks back at *Mary*. "No pressure," she tells him.

Asher looks over at the two women, carefully lines up the cue ball and shoots.

Back At His Apartment

Asher wakes up the next morning... alone. "I'm glad I drank all that water when I got home last night," he says to himself. "Otherwise those four beers might have really gotten to me!" Not having a roommate gives him an immense amount of freedom, but that also means that he has no one to talk to about his problems. Talking to himself helps. "I might have won, but I also saw Mary's face. She didn't want *me*. At least I found out her real name... Emily." Suddenly exasperated, he sighs. "Now a bigger problem. 'The guys' are actually 'the girls,'" he says to himself as he stumbles out of bed. "What is *with* all these women lying to men?!" he bellows. "Or is just to me?" He sighs again. The computer grabs his attention as he walks to the kitchen. He normally chats online during breakfast, but not today. Chatting with unidentified people has been a snake in the grass, and has already bitten him once. "It won't happen twice," he says. "I won't do it."

Asher walks to the bathroom, turns the water on and talks to his reflection in the mirror, trying to accept the new stituation. "They haven't changed. They're just like guys, but they're actually girls." He half-heartedly smiles at the mirror. He suddenly bursts out, yelling at his reflection. "Oh! Who am I kidding?! They lied to *me*! They hurt *me*! After two years, I didn't *know*?! I couldn't even pick up a prostitute last night! What kind of a guy am I?!" He takes a deep breath and closes his eyes. His head sinks, and he calmly releases the air. "A nice guy," he answers himself. He raises his head again as the foggy glass begins to blur his reflection. Wiping the mirror, and sighing again, he says, "I can't help who I am. It's a curse when you're a young man and a blessing when you're an older man. I'll forgive them, but not too quick. It'll take time to regain my trust. Yeah," he says, "That sounds good. I'll tell them that."

Antarctica is unique and mysterious. Both wind and water slowly move around the continent, encircling it and making Antarctica much colder than its northern counterpart. The entire continent is constantly frozen so it can't generate clouds hefty enough to snow or even to rain. Dark for six months out of the year with practically no thunderstorms or precipitation, the entire continent is a dark desert. Since lightning and sunlight help convert breathable oxygen into ozone, there should be no mystery as to why Earth's ozone layer thins over Antarctica.

Chapter 11

Men In Black Spaceship School

Several pilots arrive in a hangar at Whiteman Air Force Base in Missouri. A folding table sits in front of rows of folding chairs arranged neatly. The table has a blue cloth covering several objects. Other folding tables sit behind the chairs, laden with coffee and doughnuts. The pilots naturally gather close to the food. They have not been told anything at all and have helped themselves to doughnuts as more pilots arrive. Soon there are dozens of pilots there, drinking coffee and talking. A man, dressed in an Osirian uniform and armor, walks toward the front. The pilots rush to take their seats. The Osirian is not as tall as General P'al - normal-sized, with short-cropped brown hair and brown eyes. After all the men have sat down, he says, "Gentlemen, my name is K'ler... and I am going to instruct you in anti-gravity flight and Faster-Than-Light physics. The first thing is that this is how our ships work. Not everyone does things the same way and sometimes not at all the same way." He speaks without much of an accent, but with abrupt words, like someone who once spoke German.

One man immediately raises his hand and asks, "Sir, why are you training us to fly *your* ships."

He straightens himself, "That is a good question, Major... Donnelly," he says. "One with a complicated answer. This is a preemptive, surprise attack," he tells them. "The rest of the galaxy needs to know that it was *you* who did it and not us."

"But why?" he asks with almost child-like curiosity. "Why would anyone believe we developed anti-gravity and Faster-Than-Light spaceships overnight?"

K'ler smirks. "Humans do amazing things all the time," he counters. The hangar murmurs with disbelief. "Anti-gravity is so simple that a man can create it in his garage, much like the first airplane. As was the automobile before that and the telegraph before that... so on and so forth. Right now there is probably some man, somewhere, that is upset because he figured it all out and we just swooped in one day and beat him to it! That happens more often than you realize."

Major Donnelly looks around a little then asks, "I understand what you're saying about invention, but what do you mean about the rest of the galaxy and us?"

"The entire galaxy," he begins, "has known about Humanity for a long time. Lemurians, Reticulans and others all evolved from one of the first animal groups on their planet, the arthropods. Having such an *ancient* form, you would probably think those aliens look alike... and they do. Since evolution ENDS once sentience BEGINS, they never evolved beyond short, gray creatures with blue blood."

Another man raises his hand and stands up, fidgeting nervously. "Sir. First of all, what does *sentience* mean? And second, do you mean they *literally* have blue blood?" he asks before sitting down as fast as he can.

K'ler looks at the floor, then raises his head before answering. "Sentience means *consciousness or self-awareness.* And yes," he tells the young man, "their blood is literally blue. It is based on copper."

"Shouldn't it be green?" he asks from his chair.

K'ler laughs quietly. "You watch too much television," he tells him, then says to the whole group, "Their blood is based on copper two, not copper one. They breathe oxygen, just like you do and breathable oxygen is two. There are *many* species of short, gray aliens. They have been around for millions and millions of years. Sentience usually happens only once on a planet, sometimes twice. It is rare, but it happens. One time it happened three times on one planet. The people of the galaxy were absolutely amazed... until Earth. Past and present, it has happened here more than twenty times: All the whale species but none of the sharks, all the dolphin species but none of the fish, all of the elephant species but no other pachyderms, all the great ape species but none of the monkeys and so forth. That puts things in perspective, does it not?" he says. "God in Heaven has touched this planet and everyone in the galaxy knows that. God's artistry, compared to Leonardo Da Vinci's, is like comparing a Rembrandt painting to a stick drawing. There *is* no comparison. Humans are divine gifts to the *entire* galaxy. Some aliens even try to hybridize with humans, making the offspring look more like humans. There may be more or less holy places for humans, but to the rest of the galaxy *Earth* is a holy place." The group doesn't say another word. "No one in this galaxy is surprised by *anything* that humans do." He starts to change subjects but adds, "You do not realize how *close* you are to matching alien technology. All it takes is one successful man in his garage for you to begin to believe."

K'ler waits a minute or two, letting the silence dominate the mood of the hangar floor before beginning his lecture. "Okay!" he suddenly announces. "Back to the original subject!" The pilots get their pens and paper ready. "There are two major types of spaceships: those that *can* travel to other stars and those that *cannot*. You might think it is odd that some spaceships cannot travel to other stars, but think of boats or airplanes. You would not sail a rowboat to China or fly a Cessna to Africa, so why would you fly any old spaceship to Alpha Centauri? Shape is the key. Spaceships with Faster-Than-Light ability, FTL, have at least one side that is domed or shaped like a pie plate. It is more correct to think of it as a satellite dish. There is not just one big anti-gravity generator; it has many small ones. They work similar to hydrogen balloons, but with one magnifying the other. Of course, anti-gravity generators are *far* more powerful than hydrogen balloons, even though they are nothing more than rod and a tube, a piston and a cylinder. We use a substance called Stannum to line these generators, these piston and cylinder devices, to create both gravity *and* anti-gravity," he tells them. "They are *very* simple, but also very powerful. So powerful, in fact, that a soda can-sized generator can easily lift an automobile. Most of them even look like soda cans."

He removes the blue cloth and reaches for the pentagon-shaped, three-foot-wide metal panel on the table. "We also coat our spaceships with Stannum panels. He holds up the silvery panel. "Stannum is an alloy, a blend of metals, not just one. Also, there are bubbles of various gases inside the alloy, similar to your styrofoam. Is quite light." A few concentric pentagons adorn the panel. "The air bubbles expand when we apply electricity," he says, connecting two wires and a battery to it. The panel suddenly comes to life, glowing a soft blue color. The men gasp. K'ler sighs noticeably, pauses for a moment, then continues. "Different metals are blended with the Stannum to make them glow different colors. This one has selenium. Others have strontium, iron, sodium, boron, potassium or none at all. One that has no embedded metals softly glows a white color. The more power we give to it, the brighter it glows. It can look very bright at night. These panels are not necessary for flight, but they make the spaceship unique. It is similar to applying paint to an airplane. Electrified Stannum repels water like a force field," he says, squirting it with water from a spray bottle. It sprays at the panel, but seems to hit an invisible barrier several inches from the panel, then simply falls to the ground. "We can travel to *any* ocean depth without concern. When in the air, these panels are not as necessary but are still activated randomly because of water in the air. Humidity can slow a craft down more than you might realize. An activated panel next to a non-activated one looks black, just like a bright object next to a dimmer object. Sun Spots are a good example." He stops for a moment, like he just remembered something mundane. "I assume you understand that concept." The pilots clamor and tell him that they understand. "Good," he says. "People tell us that when they see these panels on our ships, the ships look like the scales of flying reptiles. That is probably where all these 'dragon' and 'flying serpent' myths come from."

"Although these panels are made of the same material, they have nothing to do with anti-gravity. A satellite dish-shaped roof makes the ship extraordinarily stable, as well. Imagine putting hundreds or even thousands of hydrogen balloons spread across and above a rowboat, then you will understand. A person will never see a spaceship lean into a turn because it does not have to do so. The Stannum walls of the spaceship protect the occupants from *any* force it endures, just like an airplane's cockpit protects a pilot from the forces that his airplane endures. The spaceship can accelerate to any speed it wants, as quickly as it wants. *There are no consequences.*"

"When the spaceship gets into space it will turn on its side." As he holds up his hands, the small silvery disk sitting on the folding table springs to life and a hologram of a UFO emerges. The pilots gasp. K'ler stops for a moment. "Your people experience wonderment with *every* technological leap forward, be it nanotube batteries or the first telephone, so it seems that I must explain this technology to you, also. A microchip in my head reads my intentions and sends them to this device," he says, picking up the disk, "by radio. It interprets my intentions as images and projects them." He sets the disk down and continues while the hologram follows his every move. It displays a UFO hovering over the 'ground' then moving up into 'space.' It turns on its side. "As I said, it will turn on its side when it gets into space. Of course, there is no such thing as *on its side* in space."

He continues, "Each generator warps only a tiny piece of space-time, but because they are arranged into the shape of a satellite dish, a paraboloid, the warping is focused through the spaceship and to that other side." The hologram highlights the right side of the ship and shows gravitational field lines, colored black, warping through the ship and to the other side. "Remember that the gravity generators are spread out, like metal in a wire mesh satellite dish. Gravity field lines can go through the spaceship, like a raindrops go through a wire mesh satellite dish. Parabolic focussing creates an artificial gravitational point on the other side of the spaceship and the spaceship 'falls' toward that point. The satellite dish-shaped roof focuses space-time just like a shaped explosive focuses explosive energy. Just like a shaped explosive, which neatly penetrates armor that normal explosives can only rip apart, the satellite dish-shaped roof focuses space-time so that the spaceship 'falls' toward a gravitational point. It can never reach the point, because the point moves as the spaceship moves."

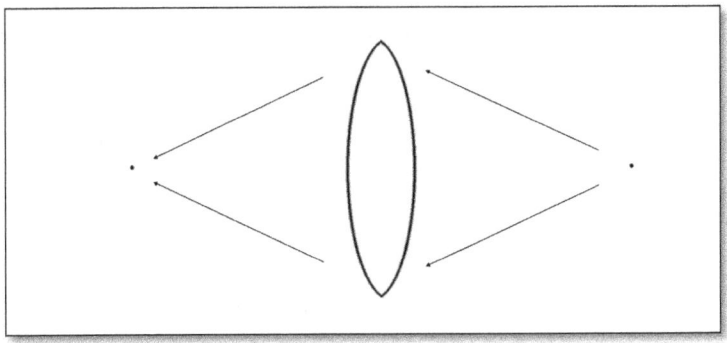

"The other side of the spaceship *also* has a satellite dish-shaped roof, but facing the opposite direction. The hologram highlights the left side of the ship this time and shows anti-gravitational field lines, colored white, warping though the ship and to the other side. "These generators do the opposite thing, as well, generating *anti*-gravity and an *anti*-gravitational field. Similar to the first side, anti-gravitational fields are focused through the ship and to a repulsion point, constantly pushing on the spaceship. One side of the spaceship is pulled while the other is pushed... and NONE of it is done with a traditional engine. It lets you reach the speed of light easily then creates a 'space-time bubble' around the spaceship, letting you break the speed of light as many times as you like." The hologram keeps pace with him, displaying the bubble and an arrow on either side, both pointing in the same direction. "One side focuses gravity and the other focuses *anti*-gravity. So one side pushes while the other side pulls. Imagine falling down a hill. Now imagine falling down that hill while you are constantly being pushed. That is what the spaceship does. The opposite space-time warps cancel each other out and you ride in a bubble of un-warped space, like riding a wave at the beach. Albert Einstein's speed limit is never broken."

Major Donnelly raises his hand again. "So is there a speed limit at all?" he asks.

"Einstein said," he replies, "If you can figure out how to break this limit once, you can break it many times over. When it is done this way, there is no limit. Foreign nationals and traders commonly travel 200 times the Speed Of Light... and far more quickly if it is needed." The pilots gasp. K'ler quietly sighs. "Getting to those speeds is not a barrier at all. The pilot simply allows room to slow down, just like an airplane lifts off, speeds up, cruises, slows down and lands."

"Like a runway?" he ventures.

"Not really," K'ler answers, "It is more like a ship in the ocean or a train on the railroad tracks allowing themselves room to slow down before they stop. Spaceships do not stop on a dime, either."

Most pilots simply clap, but others are more vocal. "Let's Roll!" and "So much for Einstein!" they shout.

K'ler holds up his hands, "Let us finish the training before you start rolling!" The group reluctantly takes their seats, but not quietly. After the murmuring dies down a little, K'ler continues, "Einstein was not wrong, but we *did* find a loophole... and there are many loopholes. This is just one of them. This information may seem complicated at first, but it is simple once you understand how it works."

Another pilot, a short, skinny man, raises his hand. "What if the UFO has a satellite dish on top but flat on the bottom?" he asks.

"Single-domed spaceships sometimes pair up," he says to the group. The hologram displays a second UFO, facing the other way. The two flat sides dock together on the flat side, looking like one spaceship with a dome on both sides. "The two flat sides dock and the principle is the same as I explained before. They can now travel Faster-Than-Light."

Major Donnelly asks, "If they understand this principle, then why do it like this? I mean, why not *only* have ships with two domes?"

"Some races do this," K'ler answers. "But most spaceships land at some point. It is easier to land if your bottom is flat than if it is curved. Of course, this is not true of all spaceships. Some spaceships never intend to land, do not care about a curved bottom or prefer to function independently and without a partner. Those are usually warships, carriers, freighters or something similar."

"Exploration ships?" a voice rings from the back.

K'ler chuckles again. "I know *your* race is new to space travel, but other races are *not*. Many alien races have been traveling in space for hundreds of millions of years. Maps are easy to acquire."

Going back to his lecture. "Putting science *fiction* aside, some spaceships may not want to travel Faster-Than-Light. They might have a short-range mission in mind and the extra speed would not help them. That is the basics of Faster-Than-Light physics and anti-gravity flight in *space*," he tells them.

"The next part of the lecture is anti-gravity flight in a planet's *atmosphere*. The atmosphere of Earth weighs 14.7 pounds per square *inch*. Flip that over and it means the atmosphere can *lift* 14.7 pounds for every square inch of an aircraft. This air pressure is able to lift a lot of weight, but not very efficiently. We use it to push our spaceships sideways, but your race can use a similar technique on their highways to push their cars with little or no gasoline."

*The Cambrian Explosion began 542 million years ago and lasted for 54 **million** years. At regular intervals, major animal types (phyla) simply appeared out of thin air, producing enormously diverse types of animals. Mollusks, Trilobites, Pikaia, Opabinia, Thectardis, Charnia and many others were neither simple nor microscopic creatures. Conditions in Pre-Cambrian China exquisitely preserved fossils, but no 'ancestor fossils' exist. Most of the incredibly diverse animal life died out over the eons, and the life seen today is based on the few that survived. Darwin's theory has a dilemma.*

Chapter 12

The Plan For Mars

Asher walks into work at the Eisenhower Building and is immediately greeted by a man in a familiar uniform. Wearing black battle armor with the black overside and blue underside cape, he is dressed like General P'al... but not as tall. *He must be in the Osirian army,* Asher thinks. His cape only drapes to his thighs and not the floor. Asher can tell by the two silver bars on his collar that this man is a captain.

Asher steps back, wondering what he did wrong, when the Osirian officer strikes his heart with his right fist, pauses for a half a second, then bows. *I guess that was an Osirian salute,* he thinks. Standing again he says, "I salute you in the name of the Cherubim. I am Captain T'rell. I bring an important message from L'lith."

Asher shakes the last bit of *sleepy* out of his head. "Am I in some sort of trouble?" he asks.

The man laughs. "If you were 'in some sort of trouble,'" he says, "I'd have brought a contingent of armed soldiers." Asher glances around to see if there are any soldiers. Seeing no one lurking in the shadows, he decides that it must be some sort of soldier-humor. "L'lith is impressed with you and wants to see you!"

Trying to avoid the situation, he points to the computer lab. "I... I've got to get to work," he says.

The Osirian captain doesn't skip a beat. "That's already been cleared," he replies. He steps aside and extends his hand toward the hallway. "If I may," he says, almost insistently.

Realizing he has no choice in the matter, he timidly says, "Okay," and follows the captain's lead. "Thank you," he remembers to add. Captain T'rell nods and walks toward the hallway. Even with the captain's word that he was not doomed, Asher still has knots in his stomach as they walk to L'lith's newly assigned office in the White House.

"Mr. Asher!" L'lith exclaims as Asher and Captain T'rell enter the room. Behind her, a very large Osirian flag dominates the huge room: Dolphins and humpback whales swim in a circle with a solid, light blue background. The heavy wooden desk displays marble carvings of blue whales. Its chair looks more like a throne, and a very large man stands in the back of the room... General P'al.

Captain T'rell salutes again. "My Lady," he says, bowing lower this time.

He remains bowed while she tells him. "Thank you, Captain. You're dismissed." Still bowed, he backs away, leaving the room.

She walks around the desk and shakes Asher's hand with both of hers. "Should I call you Jonathan, Mr. Asher or just Asher?"

"It doesn't matter," he says, with her still holding his hand. "I'll answer to any of them." However her eyes seem to demand an immediate answer, "Asher," he offers politely.

"It's good to meet you, Asher," she says, then drops his hands. "I am L'lith." She motions to the corner, "This is General P'al."

Still timid, "Yes. I remember both of you," he answers.

"Now Asher," she begins, "You are a very valuable person to *all* of us." L'lith slowly walks to her desk as she speaks. "Your mind is as good or better than any of our best people." Asher feels flattered. "We want to encourage you and to cultivate those like you," she says as she sits down.

Emotion pours into him. "Ma'am, I cannot express the honor I feel right now."

She holds up her hand at first, but decides not to comment... yet. She lowers it again and continues. "It gets better," L'lith says with a smirk. "As you know, we have Faster-Than-Light and gravitational technologies. I also know that you and your people have been interested in Mars for quite some time." Asher nods. "We would like *you* to head a terraforming project on Mars."

Asher could **not** have beeen more excited! *An actual terraforming project,* he muses. He had daydreamed about turning Mars into an Earth-like planet for years, but actually *doing it* is something else.

"We will show you how to increase Mars' gravity, how to bring water to the planet and even how to coalesce the two small moons." Asher looks pensive, like he has a question. L'lith answers him before he can ask the question, "Hephaes will do the physical labor and no, this isn't a temporary thing," she says. "Asteroid iron is heavier than most people realize and there is more iron in one of the larger asteroids than has been mined in all of human history. The Asteroid Belt was almost another planet; Jupiter's gravity prevented it. We'll use some of them to create a multi-point gravity field around Mars. That will raise the Martian gravity field enormously. Planets normally have a single-point gravity field."

Asher seems to understand her idea. "I thought you might be talking about those gravity generators of yours. Things that require constant maintenance, but you're not. You're talking about dropping heavy objects on Mars and naturally giving it more gravity. This method will last for... eons," he repeats to her. "The new mass of the planet will not only let humans move normally, but it'll warm the planet's atmosphere and even heat up the planet's core so it can generate a magnetic field again."

She smiles. "Precisely," she says.

Asher speaks under his breath. "I see," he says. "One of the things plants do is turn *water* into breathable oxygen. Most people think breathable oxygen comes from carbon dioxide, but that's wrong. The ice asteroids will melt and let plants grow, the plants will make breathable oxygen and people would be able to breathe normally outside of the cavern."

L'lith stands up. "Excellent, Mr. Asher!" she says.

He gets another quizzical look on his face. "But this would take... well, years," he tells her.

"Yes, it will," she answers. "In the meantime we'll build very large caverns out of the canyons. It will be like a bio-dome... a really BIG bio-dome," she emphasizes. "Mars has some really big canyons."

"Valles Marineris?!" he excitedly asks. She answers with a smile. "Oh wow!" he says, trying to contain his excitement. "That thing is huge!"

"Yes," she says. "We will use our technology to make those caverns look so much like Earth that you might not want to leave, even when it's safe to go outside. Of course, you'll have smaller houses for a number of years, but..."

"That's to be expected," he says.

She smiles again then looks away. "In 'Stage 3,' I think we will just drop those two small moons onto the surface and drag Triton over," she says, partly to herself. "A single, large moon will keep Mars from rolling around in its orbit. That'll turn it into a big gyroscope and stabilize the climate, like Earth's moon does. The two small moons may have maintained it, but they couldn't sustain more than bacteria."

Asher breaks in, "Mars will be heavier, so your people will adjust its speed. Right?"

She nods several times, "Yes. That's easy. It will be pirouetting around the solar system in no time!"

He gasps like something hit him. "Ohh!" he groans. "I didn't think about that! It'll rotate more slowly. Won't it?"

She waves her hand like she's shooing away a fly. "That's easy!" she says. "We will speed it up and make it sync with Earth." She suddenly turns around to face him. "What do you think of my offer? Do you accept?"

Asher feels elation and purpose and duty and honor and half a dozen other things all at the same time. He stands at attention. "It would be my *honor* to do this for you," he says, bowing, "My Lady." He leaves a few minutes later in complete elation. This has been his best day EVER!

After Asher leaves, General P'al speaks. "Was that a good idea?"

L'lith answers calmly, "Yes. This will put the non-combative humans in debt to us and keep them out of the way at the same time." She sighs. "I hate to say this, P'al, but the fate of our kind depends on their survival... at least some of them."

Later that day, Asher sits at a table in the same coffee house, waiting for the two girls. He fidgets in his chair, not able to hold still and looking like he's been drinking coffee all day. The other customers take notice, wondering if he is an escaped convict or a paranoid lunatic or something. The employees think he just had too much coffee and ignore him.

Tex and Joanne walk into the shop a few minutes later. He stands up quickly, "You won't believe the news, you guys!" he blurts. "Come sit! Sit!" He motions toward chairs at the table and sits down... partially. The girls slowly approach the table, wary of his mood the night before, but sit down just the same.

Tex speaks first, "Last night you were crushed when you saw us. Now you're about to jump out of your skin." Whispering, "Have you taken something?"

He shakes his head, laughing quietly. Making a concerted effort to contain his excitement. "I've been given something," he says, "but not a drug."

The two girls look at each other, back to him and then press closer. He chokes down another laugh. "I'll start from the beginning," he says, still fidgeting. "Last night I was crushed. I walked home in *complete* self-pity. This morning I tried to forget that you two had lied to me, but I just couldn't do it."

Joanne interrupts. "We're so sorry," she says.

"I know," he says quickly, brushing the apology aside and drawing in a deep breath. "I've decided to forgive the two of you, but things will be different for a while."

Joanne looks relieved. "We weren't sure you'd forgive us," she says. "I'm not sure *I* would have."

Tex looks at her. "Speak for yourself," she says. "I was sure. For one, he's a nice guy. For two, he's a north-easterner. They'll believe anything, true or not."

Joanne groans. "You and your 'north-easterner garbage!' You know you're in the middle of the northeast. Right?"

Smiling. "I know," she says. "I'm just messing with him." She sees the serious look on Asher's face and stops.

"Sorry," she says. "I meant the 'nice guy part' a lot more." She takes an uncomfortable breath. "You were saying?"

He huffs. "When I went into work this morning, I was greeted by an Osirian captain.

Tex gasps. "Oh crap. That big guy?"

"Not yet," he says. "This was a 'normal-looking' guy that took me to see that big guy and L'lith herself."

The girls gasp and in unison, say, "OH CRAP!"

Joanne asks, "What did you do?"

Asher can't help but smile. "I listened to her," he says, trying *hard* not to give it away.

"What did she want?" Tex asks.

"She had an offer for me," he tells her. The two girls look at each other, then back to him. "She wants *me* to head up a project to colonize Mars and terraform it," he says, with an enormous smile.

Joanne jumps up from her seat and screams, "OH MY GOD!" Everyone in the coffee house immediately looks at them, but she could not care less. Amazingly, Asher is the calmest of the three now. She takes in a deep breath, holds her hands to her heart and lets the breath out slowly. "You're doing it, Asher," she tells him. "You're doing it. I knew you could. I knew it!"

Still in her chair, Tex leans over to him, "Emperor Asher, you know my real name is Erin. Right?" He turns his head to face hers and nods.

Without uranium deposits nearby or modern nuclear testing, an ancient city in southern Pakistan shows strong evidence of a nuclear blast: Vitrification of clay walls, severe radiation sickness in human remains and high radiation levels in the soil. Several ancient cities in India have similar characteristics. The Mahabharata, *an ancient Indian epic, describes three glowing metal cities firing weapons "charged with all the power of the universe" at each other - a battle of the gods. It almost sounds like Mohendro Daro and other cities were unfortunate casualties.*

Chapter 13

Terraforming Begins

General P'al's silvery, cigar-shaped craft streaks away from the blue-green glow of Earth and into the blackness of space. "Mars is one hour," he tells his three guests. He doesn't lift a finger, but several maps and charts flash across the view-screen.

Asher looks at him. "Why so short?" he asks.

General P'al misses the point of the question. "A vimana is slow," he says without looking at him. "Their domes are not big," he says, pointing to the front and rear of the ship.

"Space-time warping is small." The flashing view-screen stops, and he turns around. "The course is programmed. Forty-three minutes."

The vimana orbits around Mars to its far side. A cube hovers in space, silhouetted against the planet's brownish-red glow. Asher had not seen the cube against the blackness of space, but also notices that it isn't a true cube. Looking like a box that is over-full and about to burst, it's bowed on two opposite sides. Asher wonders why. As the ship grows in the view-screen, he sees that the cube is larger than he thought... much, much larger. He also realizes it's not a silhouette at all. The enormous cube is midnight-black, looking like something out of an Arthur C. Clarke story. Amidst the excitement, Asher feels a cold chill run down his spine. *Why does this ship fill me with forboding?* he wonders.

"This is the *Ares*," he tells the threesome. "A storage vessel."

Asher, Joanne and Erin stare at the titanic vessel floating in front of them. Erin speaks first, "I thought it would be cooler-looking."

Asher defends the vessel, like it's his duty now. "There is no air in space, so there are no aerodynamic advantages to a 'cool-looking' ship. There's certainly no extra room, either! If you want to store something, you put it in a box. That's what they did."

"I still think it should look cooler," she almost pouts.

Asher estimates the cube as more than two *miles* in any direction. He remembers how tiny he felt, the awe of standing underneath G'brael's giant ship. He doubts this is the only ship of this size, and now knows that G'brael's ship is fairly small, by comparison. Of course, that's like saying the Rocky Mountains are small, compared to the Himalayas. General P'al, unattracted by the majestic sight in front of him, simply pilots the silvery craft between the landing bay doors at the rear corner of the massive ship.

Dim lights greet them inside the landing bay, and the doors close behind them. The foursome steps out of the vimana and into the docking bay. Erin sniffs the air before walking to the far end of the bay. The sliding metal doors open automatically and they walk between them and into a pitch-black room. A single, dim light comes to life directly in front of them, revealing a figure standing only a few feet away. Joanne shrieks, but only for an instant. General P'al looks down at her and frowns. "Sorry," she says. "It startled me."

Another light ignites, revealing several more figures, then another and another and another... The massive assemly of figures stand in formation like soldiers at attention. Their 'skin' is the color of a Caucasian man's and their hair is made of thin necklace chains, colored for effect. Their bodies are draped in a brownish, chain mesh garments. Some figures even have 'beards' and different colors of 'hair.' The effect is surprisingly realistic.

General P'al walks, takes a few steps forward, then pivots to face the group. He motions toward the figures. "These are the Hephaes. Construction robots. They don't need air. They don't need food. They don't need water. They don't need sleep. They don't need light," he tells them. "They work quickly. Radiation-proof. Thirty more rooms of them."

Asher is impressed. "Even at only a dozen feet away, I doubt I could tell the difference between this robot and a human, especially if it moves," he tells General P'al. "We have mannequins that look as human as these look, but we can't make anything walk on two legs very well."

General P'al looks at him. "Two legs aren't hard. Use humans as models." He takes a noticeable breath. "Physical therapists know. Not a lunge. Not a controlled fall. The robot must weight-shift. Move weight onto each leg. Explain to engineers."

He then leads them to a basic elevator, taking them to one of the lower floors. "Do not move fast," he tells them. "Floor gravity plates. Set to minimum. Sense your presence. Increase around you. Decrease when gone. Floor plates are not smart," he says, pointing to his head. The elevator and each floor lacks a door, allowing Asher to see a light illuminating a single robot, marking the corner of yet another vast warehouse. The single illuminated robot reminds Asher of the thousands upon thousands of robots next to it. *An army of master craftsmen,* he imagines.

Erin taps on General P'al's armored arm. "When can they start?" she asks.

General P'al gives her a menacing look. She immediately backs away and puts her hands to her sides. The group continues to descend through 30 floors. They come to a very, *very* tall room. Asher can see the face of a giant model of a Hephaes from the elevator. As they continue to descend, he sees the body, then finally the feet before coming to a halt.

General P'al motions to them. "Right this way," he says in his usual ultra-deep voice. Asher and the girls slowly walk off the elevator. The girls are awe-struck. "Whoa!" Erin exclaims. "Is this a model of the others?" Just then, another light blinks into life, revealing two more of the giant figures. Other lights blink into life, revealing even more giants.

Colossal icons now surround them, each about 15 stories tall. Asher turns to General P'al. "These aren't models. Are they?" he asks, as if it was a statement.

"No," P'al replies. "These are giant Hephaes. They do the heavy work. Small ones do the details." Lights continue to ignite. Through his White House attachments, Asher has seen big warehouses before. Each was awe-inspiring, but this warehouse is big enough to have its own weather system.

Asher looks up at it, feeling minuscule next to it. "My God," Joanne says, as if she saw the titanic machines just now. Asher looks over at her. He'd forgotten she was there. Smiling, she looks at him. "It's like standing next to the Statue of Liberty," she says. Looking up at the giant robot, "but this one moves. I can only imagine what it can do." Lights continue to spring to life in the far, far distance. They can now see the vast numbers of these titanic machines at their disposal.

General P'al turns to face Asher. "Use the Martian canyons. Get asteroid iron. Four iron layers. Put soil between layers. Squeeze until it is rock. A foot at the bottom. Build man-made caverns. Build the houses inside. Faster assembly time. Make them pretty later," he says. "Caverns protect humans. Falling asteroids. Cosmic radiation. Carbon dioxide. The cold air outside."

Erin pipes in. "How is a little cold bad for you?" she asks. "Russians do it all the time."

Asher turns to her. "There are several orders of magnitude difference," he tells her. "It is *so cold* outside that most of the air has frozen and fallen to the ground."

Realizing that she's doesn't know much about this stuff; she quietly utters, "Oh," and backs away.

"The surface will take time," General P'al tells her, unusually nicely. "Live underground for now. It will protect you."

Joanne also tries to flex her mental muscles. "What about domes?" she asks.

Asher thinks about it for a minute. General P'al seems uncomfortable. "No," Asher announces. "They'll be dropping comet-sized chunks of ice all over the planet. These are *really big* pieces of ice. Even the strongest domes can't survive ice that is a hundred times the size of a *glacier* falling on it."

"Oh," she says, looking down. "I guess you didn't need us after all."

Asher moves to hold Joanne's hands. "Not at all," he says. She looks up at him, and Erin quietly backs away. "Mars may be about a third the size of Earth, but it's far from small. We could build domes far away from any falling ice, but there's also the temptation to go outside, especially when the sky begins to appear blue."

Joanne looks into his eyes. "You want to protect people," she says.

Looking down at her, "Yes," he says. "Otherwise we'd have to black out the domes so people couldn't see the sky, the ocean or the green plants. There wouldn't be much of a point..."

Joanne breaks away from him. "You *almost* had it," she says. "You say sweet, wonderful things... then you keep going... saying 'not so sweet' things. Ugh! You're frustrating!" Asher just stands there, not understanding at all.

Erin steps in, "I understand her point." "It's a *small* point," she says, glaring at Joanne for a moment, "but it's a point. Think of a woman as a different species from a man... let's say a cat. You wouldn't lure a cat with a pizza. You might think a pizza is good, but a cat doesn't. You'd use something the *cat* thinks is good: Tuna fish, a saucer of milk, catnip. The same thing is true of a woman. *She* likes different things that you do: Nice fragrances, soft lotions, sweet words. Most of all, a woman likes to see her man being strong."

Frustrated, General P'al suddenly asks, "Will this plan work for you?"

Asher snaps out of his daze. "Yes," he says. "It's fine. Go ahead with it."

"Need a saucer of milk?" he goads.

Asher glares at him. "No... thank you," he replies. "We're done here, anyway."

General P'al briskly leads them back to the elevators. They ascend in silence and continue to walk briskly back to the shuttle. "Not good to bring females."

Asher stops, "Wait!" he yells. General P'al stops and turns around. "They don't deal with you at all. These are *my* advisors. They are with *me*. They are *my* responsibility, and not yours."

General P'al huffs, turns around and walks vigorously back to the shuttle. Erin leans over to Asher's ear. "Nicely done," she says. He smiles at her and the threesome dash off to catch up with General P'al.

Six Hours Later

Under a frosted white sky, two figures walk single-file, carrying a glistening column on their shoulders. Looking like beasts of burden and only covered with simple clothing, they heft a column as thick as a man's waist and nearly two men long across a barren plateau. Hephaes. They walk toward an *immense* canyon, looking like a gaping wound in the desert, now being healed by an enormous spider web-like mesh. Strange. A second robot pair approaches them, lugging another column. A third pair joins them, then a fourth and then a fifth.

The 150-foot-tall robots make the 15,000-ton columns look small, but the vast canyon dwarfs them both. Fallen asteroids litter the desert. Hundreds of robots form long lines, moving away from the massive meteorites and toward the canyon, like ants from a long forgotten sandwich. Other robots make long 'shafts' by taking the columns, laying them sideways and welding them together with powerful lasers. They work each shaft into the sider web-like mesh, creating a tighter and tighter iron frame, like a rebar frame inside a concrete mold. Asher sees that the columns have holes inside, making them more like pipes than columns. Anti-gravity braces prevent these enormous pipes from collapsing to the canyon floor.

The foursome watch the scene on a view-screen from the safety of the shuttle. General P'al speaks for the first time in several hours with his usual ultra-low voice and in his strange speech pattern. "From your Asteroid Belt," he says, pointing to the enormous meteorites littering the ground. "Convenient. A blast can break orbit. Then correct its fall. Time is a factor. We used heavy freighters. These have soft-landed. These have not burned-up. These have not broken. Some canyons are big here. This is the biggest one. Brought the resources here. They have good iron. Make into iron frames. The frames are vaulted. Each frame is a layer. There are four layers. Two hundred feet of dirt. Dirt between the layers. Each layer has smaller vaults." He closes his eyes and takes another breath. "Gravity Generators. Anti-gravity Braces. Squeeze until it is rock. Build man-made caverns."

"It will be a cross between a dome and a Roman aqueduct." Asher says.

General P'al looks at him. "Domes are round," he tells him. "This is not." He looks back at the screen.

"Then it's more like a Gothic vaulted ceiling," he says again, pushing his luck.

Erin laughs. "That's a relief!" she says. I thought you were talking about vaults of money!"

"So did I," Joanne admits. The girls laugh. "I wondered how that was going to help us!"

General P'al menacingly glares at the two of them, and they immediately stop laughing. "Yes," he answers, turning back to the screen and quietly taking a deep breath. "We will cover last frame. Two hundred feet of dirt."

Erin gasps. "Four vaults and two hundred feet each? That's eight hundred feet!" Erin asks. "Is there enough room?"

General P'al smiles for the first time since… ever. "Plenty," he tells her. "Twenty thousand feet deep."

She sheepishly utters, "Oh," and works her way behind the others.

General P'al continues, "The result is flat ground. It will look like the rest."

Asher turns to him, "Why do we need that?"

"You never know," he replies. "Falling ice asteroids. Would be from us. It might be enemy ships. You never know. Hide your house well. You can do what you want." Asher nods in agreement. "Fifteen thousand tons each," General P'al says. "Only 6,000 tons now. Gravity is not fixed. That is Stage Two. Twenty-five feet wide. Two fifty feet long."

Erin's eyes bulge. "That's almost as long as a football field!" she exclaims.

"The Hephaes make the pieces look a lot smaller," Asher tells her.

General P'al doesn't care. "Yes," he growls. "The small Hephaes fix flaws. After more asteroids. We will start on Stage 2."

Erin whispers to Joanne. "It is just me or does this remind you of the iron bars of a prison and being buried alive?" Joanne turns to her, and gives her a 'knowing' nod. Both girls cling to hope, but have their doubts about this project.

Federal does NOT *mean national. It's just called by its original description. A federal system holds one state to laws written by its people. A national system holds every state to laws written by other people. The current system thinks everyone is the same, which is like saying that since every road is practically the same, every speed limit should be the same no matter where it's located.*

Chapter 14

Come To Mars!

"Christian, traveling to Mars is *easy* now," Asher tells the well-known TV host on a split-screen interview. "With Osirian spacecraft, we can get there in a couple of hours. With our own technology, it would take more than two years to get there! Amazing! Right?!"

The TV host simply looks at him with pity and remorse. "I hear it's a wasteland there," he says. "No air. No life. Bitterly cold. You'd better pack your Long Johns."

Asher laughs. "Colder than that," he says. It's so cold there that the carbon dioxide atmosphere has frozen out of the air, laying on the ground near the poles. Most of what's left is just vapor that has sublimed. It doesn't matter, because we'll live underground, anyway. We'll have all the air and heat we want."

The interviewer rolls his brown eyes, like he's making a joke. "We'll be cavemen, again! Won't we?"

"Not caves, Christian, man-made caverns. I've seen one myself. Mars has some *really* big canyons. The first one is over two thousand miles long and a hundred miles wide."

"WOW!" he exclaims. "That's pretty big!"

The host's graying blond hair refuses to move. "They're not *all* that big, but the first one is."

"We probably won't need another!" the host injects.

Asher ignores him. "Giovanni Schiaparelli said there were 'grooves' on Mars, but the Italian word is 'canali.' Add 'Americanization' to imagination and you get 'Percival Lowell seeing canals on Mars.' *Planet-wide* terraformation will take quite some time, so the Osirians will turn that enormous canyon into a human bio-dome. They will dig it even deeper, then put a huge roof on it. Trillions of tons of asteroid iron and soil serve as the cavern's roof and it will be filled with breathable oxygen. Afterwards, the construction robots build human houses inside these caverns. They are extremely fast builders! In the meantime, we are protected from 'Stage 2.'"

"I almost afraid to ask," he says. "What's 'Stage 2'?"

"Gravity," he replies. "Gravity is the key, Christian," he says. "With 260% more gravity, the wispy atmosphere will fall to the surface, like it does here. It does it there, too, but Mars doesn't have enough gravity to do it very well. Molecules of air will bump into each other and warm the air a little, like it does here. The ice caps and other frozen water will melt into rivers and lakes. Some will evaporate and join the air, bumping into other atmospheric gases and warming them a little more. The Osirians will bombard Mars with ice and nitrogen asteroids, which will melt into oceans, like it did here. It'll take a long time or never, if Nature melts the ice, so lasers fired from orbit will speed up the process. Some of the melted ice will evaporate and warm the air a little more, while water vapor and carbon dioxide will give Mars a Greenhouse Effect, like it does here."

Christian looks disturbed. "Isn't that bad?" he asks.

Asher knew this question would come up. "Not at all," he answers. "Do you know which greenhouse gas is both the strongest *and* the most abundant?" Christian gives him a quizzical look. "Water vapor," he says.

His jaw drops. "You're kidding me!" he says. "I thought for sure it was carbon dioxide!"

"Not even close," Asher tells him. "Carbon dioxide isn't 0.3% of our atmosphere or even 0.03%. It's 0.003% of our atmosphere. Miniscule. And it's the *weakest* of the four major greenhouse gases. Earth is so far from the sun, that it can't warm our planet by itself. The Greenhouse Effect compounds the sun's heat. Earth would be a frozen *wasteland* without the greenhouse effect."

Christian tries to challenge Asher's comments, "What about Venus and its run-away Greenhouse Effect?"

Asher looks at him like he's stupid. "There are *several* orders of magnitude difference," he says. "Venus is close to the sun *and* it spins very, very slowly *and* it has 3,200 times more carbon dioxide in its atmosphere, *and* there's about 90 Earth atmospheres of pressure. The air pressure is so massive that it'd crush a human to the size of a soda can in less than a second. Should I go on?"

Christian blows off the whole thing with a child-like laugh. "Well I can see that you're one of those really smart people that enjoys all that science stuff."

Asher manages a laugh. Idiot, he thinks. All he has to do is look in a book instead of believing everything he sees on TV. He quietly takes a deep breath. 'Calm down,' he tells himself. Calm down. We're in two separate studio sets. At least he can't spray me with spittle.

"It almost sounds too easy," Christian says. "Why hasn't this been suggested before?"

"There are two answers for your two questions," he said. "It's easy because of Osirian technology and, yes, it has been proposed before."

"I know that the second Bush proposed it, but I don't remember anyone else saying it."

Asher feels more comfortable now. "You're pitching to my strengths, Christian. A mission to Mars and eventual colonization of Mars has been floating around the Capitol since the Apollo missions in the 70's. NASA even wrote a proposal in 1989. Unfortunately it was a 450 billion dollar side of pork."

"Nixon?" Christian asks like a statement.

"Not really," Asher smiles for a moment, but becomes serious again. "In 1990 an independent engineer proposed a viable and achievable mission that would get men on Mars by 1999. It received a wonderful response then suddenly fizzled.

The second Bush tried to revive it, but it wasn't handled well. The problem is that big projects take ten or more years to accomplish. Presidents come and go in that period of time, and it only takes one idiot with an expensive domestic agenda to mess it all up."

Completely ignoring Asher, "That sounds like Congress," he says. "But seriously," he says, "are you talking about astronauts going to Mars or a colony for real people?"

"A colony," Asher says quickly. *Idiot!* he screams in his mind. *I just told you that!* "With Osirian spacecraft and construction robots, large habitats can be constructed in a matter of weeks and ready before anyone even shows up."

Christian smirks. "Robots don't need oxygen. Do they?" he says, letting out another unnerving laugh. With that, Asher's segment is over, the studio's director motions for him to get off of the set and the show soon ends. After a few pleasantries Asher ducks out through the back door of the studio, happy to make an escape.

Back At His Apartment

Asher watches part of the digital broadcast of L'lith's comments on his computer. It's the part that mentions the magnetic pole shift. He does a quick 'search' on the Internet, and looks at a map of where the magnetic pole has been since about 1450. "Records of the magnetic north pole have been kept longer than I realized," he says, talking to himself out loud. It helps him to think. "It looks like the magnetic north pole has meandered around the same area for centuries," he says, looking at the map carefully. "It has made a couple of U shapes, but began to pick up speed about... the mid-1980's. Since then it has been making a beeline for Earth's *rotational* North Pole."

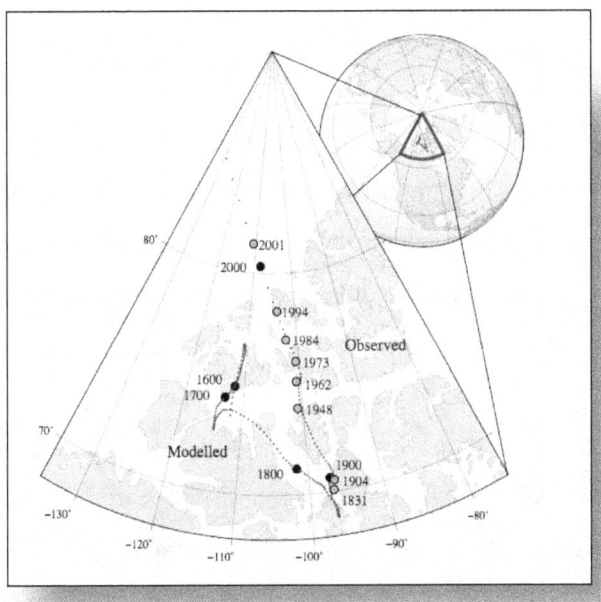

He sits back in the computer chair, and rubs the tiny bits of stubble on his chin with his fingers. "Hmm... L'lith said that the pole shift will be caused by human activity, but she didn't say *which* activity. Knowing politicians, it's probably the *opposite* of what we think." He continues to rub at the tiny bits of stubble. "I know that Earth is *not* getting warmer. It's getting cooler." Thinking silently for a few minutes, he moves his hand to the side of his face, and rubs the tiny bits of stubble over there. "Humans have been using less, burning less and generally emitting less carbon dioxide, because of the 'Global Warming' craze, and it's getting cooler as a result." Asher sits up in the chair. "A cooler Earth means there is more ice and less seawater, since the ice in seawater is freshwater. Slow freezing extracts freshwater from saltwater. Earth has wobbled for 4 ½ billion years, because there is more landmass in the northern hemisphere than in the southern hemisphere. And since ice is lighter than water, and *way* lighter that seawater, the weight will shift and the wobbling will slow down." On roll now, he stands up. "Yellowstone Park's supervolcanic eruption would make things a *lot* worse," he says to himself. "It took a *century* for Earth's average temperature to warm up after Mount Tambora's supervolcanic eruption in 1815, and Yellowstone is bigger. Mount Tambora killed thousands, and crippled enormous empires when it spewed 38 cubic miles of ejecta. *That* was the biggest eruption is human history. Yellowstone can spew *240* cubic miles!" Focusing on the magnetic poles again, "The Earth's rotation will drive the *magnetic* north pole to the *rotational* North Pole. When it gets there, it'll spin around like it's in a washing machine's spin cycle, and get flung almost halfway down the planet!"

Asher sits down again, and continues to talk to himself. "'Water is weakly diamagnetic, and will follow the magnetic field,'" he says, quoting L'lith. "If the magnetic north pole is in Arizona, then the magnetic *south* pole..." He looks at some maps on his computer. "Sedona is 34.8° North by 111.7° West, so it'll be 34.8° South by 68.3° East, the southern Indian Ocean." He looks again to check his math. "Hmm... Half of the seawater will move toward the new *north* pole, and half will move to the new *south* pole. Which means the Gulf of Mexico will grow... until it splits our country in two. The Mediterranean Sea will drain, and Japan will be completely submerged." He stops playing with stubble, and puts his hands on the chair's armrest. "Damn! She's right!"

The U.S. Justice system has become so bungled that if a person kills a sitting Senator and is actually *convicted, the Justice System will give him a prize. He will get to spend years in safe and clean housing without any expenses: Rent, food, electricity or clothing. Even health care is free. In the odd chance that he goes to death row, it would be at least eight years before that happens, and it's closer to 15 or 20 years in northern states. An older person might even die of natural causes first! By definition, a good person obeys the rules of civilized society. A bad person doesn't obey any rules at all, so evil will always triumph over good. That is, unless the good person sees this loophole, and decides to double tap him in the head.*

Chapter 15

The Fleet Begins To Move

A heavy freighter floats in high Earth orbit, looking like a squashed ball bearing and concealing eight attack ships tucked inside its smooth, silvery shell. The teardrop-shaped hulls of the attack ships can't fly into deep space on their own, but they can certainly launch an attack. Each is armed to the teeth with one hundred nuclear missiles. Like a piece of bread from a giant toaster, each attack ship is loaded backwards, ready to spring out of its slot at a moment's notice. Twenty-seven of the freighter's brethren float in orbit near the first freighter.

Some of the fleet still haven't closed their accordion-like space doors, while nearly *three thousand* nuclear missiles wait for a single command.

"Be sure to attack their oceans, too," L'lith reminds a ship pilot. "They live on the land *and* on the ocean floor."

"Yes, Ma'am," the ship's pilot replies. "I remember." L'lith pauses for a minute, looking at the man, then turns and walks away. The pilot waits until she is out of earshot before saying, "I may just be an Air Force pilot, but I'm smart enough to listen and follow instructions." The co-pilot gives an absent-minded nod, then continues checking readings in the ship's cockpit.

A few minutes later, a small, silvery craft emerges from the giant freighter. Barely visible, L'lith's descent may as well have been a flea jumping off the side of a German Shepherd. The craft descends toward the Earth and disappears. The freighter's forward view-screen transfers to each attack ship and each pilot watches as the last of the space doors all begin to close. One by one, the enormous freighters slowly begin moving away, heading 'south' of the solar system. They seem to plod slowly at first, but within minutes they are as far away as the moon. The Earth and its moon grow smaller and smaller until everything suddenly disappears. "We've reached the Speed of Light," he tells the co-pilot. "Light can't catch up to us anymore. We are just passengers inside of a bullet now."

"I don't feel any differently at all."

"K'ler said it'd be like this," the pilot replies.

"I know," he says. "But it's still amazing"

The freighter accelerates faster and faster. The stars look like points of light, quickly moving toward it, but as the ship gets closer, they streak, like on TV. Unlike TV, though, the streaking stars vanish as the freighter passes them. There's a reason why is called a Faster-Than-Light drive! Only the navigational computer guides them, which now reads 'Fifteen C'!

The same attack ship pilot yells with excitement. "Fifteen times the Speed of Light!" he roars. "Can you believe we're actually going that fast?!"

The co-pilot shrugs. "How do we slow down?" he asks calmly.

"The computer will switch the gravitation and repulsion fields at the midpoint and we'll decelerate the rest of the way," the pilot answers, calming down. "K'ler said this is an emergency flight, so we'll get close to a *thousand* times the

Speed of Light by the time we reach the midpoint. They've made these things as easy to fly as driving a car."

"I don't remember switching gravitational fields in the owner's manual of my Pontiac," the copilot says sarcastically.

"Yeah," he answers, perplexed by his indifference. "Well... we accelerate until we reach the halfway point, then switch the fields and decelerate for the other half. The Osirians gave us a crash course on stellar navigation before we were allowed to come up."

"No pun intended. Right?" he says. "A crash course?"

The pilot 'gets it' and chuckles. "Yeah," he says. "The fleet separates and comes at the planet from four directions, like it's a four-sided pyramid."

"You mean a 'tetrahedral attack pattern,'" he says. The co-pilot looks forward again and says, "That's a good plan."

Still confused by the man. "Yeah," he says, bewildered. He snaps out of it. "There are four groups: Alpha, Beta, Gamma and Delta. Seven freighters to a group, the group will get into position, they'll launch the attack ships... us, we launch the nukes, the aliens go 'bye-bye' and we go back home." He drops into his chair. "Simple," he adds, putting his feet up. "Just the way I like it."

"It's a long way to the Reticulan homeworld and we have another fifteen hours before we get to the halfway point and switch the fields," the co-pilot says, standing up. "I'm going to the galley. Do you want me to get you anything?"

"I don't suppose we have any beer up here?" he asks.

The co-pilot walks down the hallway. "Not likely," he replies. "I'll need a stiff drink tonight... or two or three."

Spinning around in his chair. "I might join you. Do you think they have any beef jerky around here?"

The Colony Is Almost Finished

Asher walks around one of the newly built Martian apartment complexes. The cavern that the Hephaes built for human colonists is larger than he thought. They have sculpted the interior of a dome into the rock and engineered it somehow. Impressive illusions of dawn, daylight, dusk and night appear under the dome. *Humans feel less stressed when they can see the sky,* he thinks and walks into one of the apartments. *I know they're speeding up Mars' day length to match it with Earth's,* he thinks to himself. The apartment isn't finished, but looks like it will be about the size of a typical bedroom on Earth. Tiny. *It will suffice,* he decides. *After all, this IS the FIRST colony.* He breathes deeply a few times. *The air is good,* he smiles. He jumps up and nearly hits his head on the ceiling before trickling back to the floor. *But the gravity still lacks a little,* he groans. *The gravity is better than it was before we started, but it'll get even better when the ice asteroids get here.*

A familiar voice comes from the doorway. "Is it what you hoped for?" Asher whirls around to see G'brael standing in the open doorway.

Stunned for a moment, "Yes," he says blankly. Asher gathers himself. "I wasn't sure if I'd see you again."

G'brael moves into the room. "I wanted to congratulate you. Deceiving the Osirians and making them work for you is no small accomplishment."

Asher looks confused, "I don't understand what you mean, G'brael. We didn't deceive anyone. The Osirians are helping us to survive a disaster."

"Well," he says, "your superiors might not have told you about the deception." He looks around the room. "Small homes are fine. High populations or multicultural societies are fine. Just be sure to spread out the city, and give the people more room. Too many people living in one area damages the entire society."

"Damages?" he asks. "Are you talking about vandals?"

G'brael turns around to face him. "Oh no," he says. "Not that kind of damage. Just the *existence* of other people irritates people... just a little bit. People are more connected than you realize. Similar people irritate the least, and extremely different people irritate the most. Multicultural societies can only work on *small* scales. The natural Amoeba Effect would create pockets of battling factions, and that's what you *don't* want. Some things just don't scale up. Especially in close quarters, *large* multicultural societies are very irritating. *Everyone* seems to understand this, except Americans. Even warlords understand this. Because there is power in numbers, *large* cities need to have similar people. The natural Amoeba Effect will create a unified society instead of a factioned society. Ethnic cleansing campaigns satisfy the warlord's need for a calmer society. He could do this simply by separating people, but that wouldn't satisfy his other need... murder. You don't want to become a warlord, so that's why I say to spread people out."

Asher nods. "That makes sense," he says. "People talk about taking a vacation, and getting away from the city all the time," he says as he puts his hand on a wall. "It's small right now, but it'll grow into a Utopia. No one will have to pay for anything."

G'brael shakes his head. "Other people have thought the way you are thinking. Socialism and communism are just survival techniques," he tells him. "They can only be used for a few years with large groups or a couple of decades with very small groups. It erodes the spirit of children... very slowly. Then it erodes *their* children's spirits... then theirs and then theirs. They might look the same, but that kind of erosion cannot be rekindled. I know. It's not a way of life." He looks down and says, "Utopia doesn't exist." Looking up again, "It can't exist," he says. "It's not that we don't want it badly enough. We do, but 'Utopia' backfires *every* time, hurting the same people you're trying to help. It doesn't matter who's 'in charge,' it's Utopia itself that doesn't work. The math backs that up."

Asher smiles at him like he doesn't know what he's talking about. "We'll figure it out. Everyone here will be smart and willing to work together."

G'brael grins and lets out a small chuckle. "They say that you should do everything when you're 18-years-old... because it's then that you know *everything*." Asher chuckles as well and looks at the ground. His body language says, *Guilty as charged!* "Seriously now, the first generation of you may be smart and willing to work together, but what about the next?"

"We're smart so our kids will be smart, too," he answers.

G'brael nods slightly. "Most maybe," he says, "but not all. There are different kinds of smart. Things like this have been tried before. What are you going to do with the ones that aren't good enough or have some sort of disability?" Asher's smile slowly evaporates. "Punish them? Force them? Banish them? Kill them? All of it has been tried before. Not everyone *can* or *should* be saved, but too much enforcement and you'll box you into a genetic corner. Too little and you'll box yourself into another corner. People will look to you... personally. You'll be the Founding Father of an entire world."

Asher looks at the floor for a minute then changes the subject. "G'brael, what did you mean about deceiving the Osirians?"

Another familiar voice comes from behind him. "Yes, G'brael. Tell us." Asher whirls around to see L'lith leaning on the door then walking into the room. General P'al also enters, ducking his head to enter the room. G'brael stands in complete silence. "Tell us," she needles him. No one utters a word as they walk into the room.

G'brael breaks his silence, "Asher, my ship is in the main hangar. Could you go there and tell the helmsman that I'll be there in a little while?" Looking at L'lith, he says, "We need to talk."

Asher feels the tension in the room. "Would you rather I just call him?" he asks timidly.

G'brael gives him a half-smile. "The cellular towers haven't been finished, yet," he says. "Have they, L'lith?"

She doesn't seem to move a muscle. "Not yet, G'brael. That's the thing about construction sites. Not everything's finished." General P'al steps aside, cueing Asher to leave the room. He reluctantly walks out of the room and General P'al closes the door behind him.

L'lith smiles and very slowly walks around G'brael. "Check and mate," she says. "I knew you'd come. You had a chance to save yourself, but didn't take it. Why? The boy?"

G'brael stands in the same spot. "He's more of a man than you realize," he says. *And he will destroy you,* he thinks. "I've lived a long life," he says. "So have you. He deserves more than his life ending right here and now."

She laughs wickedly. "You're a sentimental old fool, G'brael." She turns to P'al. "Go ahead," she says. He takes a couple of steps forward and moves his hand near his side arm. G'brael doesn't flinch at all, but takes a breath and holds it. P'al pushes a button hidden behind his side arm and his grinning face flickers like a television screen. It fades and P'al looks headless for a moment, until G'brael notices shiny, green scales where his neck had been. A serpentine neck unfolds, rising from his stomach and chest; it makes a sticky sound as it peels away, like vinyl peeling away from vinyl. P'al's *real* head emerges, released from the force-fielded and hologrammed armor. His horse-like head has the mouth and teeth of an alligator with two short, spiraled tusks jutting out of his upper and lower jaws… almost like that of a razorback hog. There is stringy, black hair on his chin and a red crest on the top of his head. P'al opens his yellow and gold-flecked eyes for the first time and the vertical slits of his pupils tighten, focusing on G'brael. G'brael takes a step back and the air in his lungs seems to disappear. There is another sticky sound as P'al bends forward. A long, alligator-like tail emerges behind him. The three, clawed fingers on his hands and the three, clawed toes on his feet spread out after enduring the force-field's constant constriction. He takes a few short breaths with his natural lungs and spreads his large form – nearly twenty feet long now. He takes a deep breath and roars like *thunder*.

G'brael finds his voice at last. "A Drakyyn!" he manages to utter. "My God!" he says to L'lith. "I thought they didn't exist anymore!"

L'lith smiles with *great* satisfaction, "Your god, G'brael? Your god has forsaken you for more than two thousand years," she tells him. "WE were the ones that brought the Drakyyn to

Earth. WE helped spread the Black Plague. WE ripped apart that stupid little country that you love so much. WE fought its creation, not the British. WE even turned some of its own citizens against it. WE are the reason they move in lock step. It's certainly not any intelligence on their part. WE turned federalism into nationalism, not Lincoln. They actually *believe* it's the same thing. A dictionary would have helped, but comprehension is not their strong suit. You call them serpents, but we call them heroes. They are mere pawns, but those pawns captured your queen. Now the Little Ice Age can continue and become a MASSIVE Ice Age. BILLIONS of people will die. That stupid little country *could* have saved everyone, but now that won't happen. We ripped it *apart*." L'lith smiles more, as if it's possible. "I guess 6,000 years of life doesn't teach you everything, G'brael. Events are already in motion. You can't stop it. You've lost," L'lith calmly says, as P'al takes another step forward.

In The Hangar

"Is that all he said?" the young helmsman asks.

Asher looks frantic. "He seemed insistent that I leave," he says.

Percival is young, Scandinavian-looking and perhaps only 21 years old. He dismisses Asher's concern. "You had me worried there for a minute," says the young helmsman. "He and L'lith may not be the best of friends, but they have known each other for... years. I doubt anything is wrong."

Still frantic, Asher asks, "Can the ship's sensors find people or monitor them or something?"

He looks puzzled by the question. "Sure," he answers. "Normally a communications officer monitors each person, except when the Council of Nine members are together. It's forbidden to monitor a Council of Nine member, but it's treason if you monitor a meeting. They take it *very* seriously. L'lith is the Osirian Council member and G'brael said she'd be here, so there was no need for a communications officer."

"What is this 'Council of Nine' thing?" Asher asks.

Percival answers, "The Council of Nine is a council of the nine leaders from each of the nine city-states," he says. "G'brael, L'lith, K'kul, R'ma, M'kul and a few others are all members."

"So he knew she'd be here," Asher thinks out loud. "He knew this would happen, too."

Still puzzled. "What would happen?" Percival asks.

197

Asher answers the question with another question. "Can you find G'brael and check his vitals?" he asks.

Percival breathes deeply and answers, "I could, but that would be a major violation of security. A Council of Nine member has more rights than ordinary citizens."

Asher sighs, "It's that way in our country, too." He looks down.

After a moment or two of silence, Percival seems to change gears. "I can locate him if I think he's in danger. Locate, but nothing more," he suddenly says.

Asher looks up. "Please, hurry! He *is* in danger," he says.

Moving toward the communications officer's corner, "Okay, now I can *genuinely* say that I am concerned for his safety!" Percival announces. He looks at the screen and wrinkles his forehead. "I don't see him immediately, but there's always some sort of interference around P'al. I'm guessing that G'brael is near him, so I'll just look for the interference." He looks for a few moments. "I found it! If I'm right, G'brael will appear on the screen when P'al walks away." Asher looks at the screen. It looks like a big smudge.

Asher asks, "Why is there always interference around General P'al?"

Never moving his eyes from the screen, "We're not *entirely* sure. Which is weird in itself," he says, giving a confused look before continuing, "but we think he's carrying some kind of high-powered weapon or something."

Curious. "Could he be a robot or a cyborg?" he asks.

"Nah," Percival answers. "Those look different. I've scanned thousands of things: Organic lifeforms, robots, cyborgs, spaceships, guns, lasers, computers, cell phones and on and on. Every species out there has a robot of themselves. I think it's a 'consciousness thing.' Anyway, we can detect every single one of them. They keep trying to beat our system, but it keeps beating them instead. We've never had to upgrade it. If you aim for the *most fundamental* things... they can't beat you. Always and forever." Percival suddenly starts talking to the screen. "What *are* you doing?" Percival mutters, as if he's talking to G'brael. "You're barely even moving."

"What about the Grays?" Asher asks. "Have you ever scanned them?"

Keeping his eyes on the screen. "Reticulans? Yeah, sure. Why?"

Mustering courage again, "I was told that they were all robots," he says.

Percival laughs and manages a sideways glance, "Who told you that?"

Asher swallows, "It came from L'lith."

"Oh!" he says, laughs again and looks back at the screen. "That's your first problem: Believing her. She's definitely a hottie but she can *lie* like nobody's business!" He steals another sideways glance. "That's not true," he says and looks back at the screen.

"So they're just a super-evolved race?" he asks.

Percival turns and looks intently at Asher, "They are NOT super-evolved," he says loudly, like he has just been insulted.

Asher cringes. "I'm sorry," he mumbles.

Percival breathes deeply for a moment then says, "No need for apologies. Evolution ends when consciousness begins. From a human's point of view, they're UNDER-volved. Their eyes are large because they're compound eyes. They have a heart and lungs combined into one organ. Ineffective. When 'one bad apple spoils the whole barrel.' One problem with either piece, and they're dead. Humans invented organ donation. Not Grays. They tried to use cattle organs once or twice. It didn't work, and they gave up. The American government has been using 'cattle mutilation' to misdirect people for *years*. A Gray's heads only seem big because his body is so small. Their brains use 'electrical synapses.' Their brain cells don't have myelin. Myelin is like insulation is to a wire, and their electrical brain cells are like bare wires. It's a very fast kind of synapse, but it's also very spread-out, so their heads are big to compensate. Grays only *appear* super-smart when they're really just a super-old race." He finally turns back to the screen. "Talk about a hornet's nest, though! The Lemurians stumbled on them millions of years ago. That simple thing started a full-scale war that lasted for centuries. That's why there's uranium on the *surface* of Earth."

"I thought it came from meteors," Asher says.

Percival still doesn't take his eyes off the screen. "Nah," he says. "There's only a grain of sand's worth of uranium in a meteor. Uranium is heavy stuff. Any uranium that fell when Earth was still molten sank into the planet's core a long, long time ago." He steals a quick sideways glance. "Mass drivers," he tells him. "Those are what drove the Lemurians underwater in the first place. That hid them from the Grays, like living underground will do for you on Mars. Remember that humans are the smartest beings in the galaxy. Answers that seem obvious to you and me, doesn't even occur to the Grays. After millions and millions of years, they STILL hold a grudge about it… and they're the ones that won the war! I think they now have two full-blown home-worlds and ten colonies."

"Twelve planets?" Asher asks. Before Percival can answer, he sees something on the screen. "It looks like I was right," he says. "P'al is leaving and G'brael's signature is emerging from the interference. G'brael is about half a mile that way." He points his finger to his right.

Asher doesn't seem happy to hear the news. "They didn't leave that room," he says. "Is he alive?"

Percival doesn't budge. "I can't," he says. He steps back from the screen. "I can't push *this button right here*," he says, pointing his finger toward a button on the screen. Asher looks at him for a moment, then walks over to the screen. "I'm not allowed to press this button," he says again, still pointing. Percival doesn't turn to look at the screen, shielding his eyes with his hand. Asher looks at the screen. *English!* he thinks and touches the button. It instantly changes, displaying his heartbeat, respiration and blood pressure.

"This doesn't look good," Asher says.

Still shielding his eyes. "Don't tell me anything about the screen," he says. "I'm still not allowed. Just tell me, 'Yes' or 'No.' Should I go to him?"

Asher nods. "Yes," he says. "I'll go with you."

Still shielding his eyes, he makes a quarter-turn. "No," he says quickly. "This is a construction site. It may not be dangerous to construction robots, but it's obviously dangerous to us humans. G'brael is *my* responsibility. You need to stay," he says and walks out the door, not letting Asher argue with him.

Asher stands motionless next to the screen. As the adrenaline subsides, denial breaks down and realization has a chance to flow into him. "She planned all this," he mutters under his breath. L'lith's endgame becomes clear. "We've been set up."

Drug cartels from Mexico regularly invade U.S. homes: Kidnapping, ransoming and even murdering residents of the U.S. Mexico is plagued with these pirates and it is not necessarily an act of war, but it's very close to it. While the U.S. government creates a true *solution, preferably a diplomatic one, California, Arizona, New Mexico and Texas National Guards could put a military presence on the international border, protecting all of the contiguous American states from this brutality. The other states could help to pay for this protection. Should drug cartels or U.S. residents have sanctuary on U.S. soil?*

Chapter 16

The Human Sneak Attack

Flying side-by-side and spread out, the enormous freighters pierce farther and farther into the into the inky blackness of deep space. The reality of the vast distances of space, even the distance between two stars, is *so* immense that a person has trouble comprehending it. Planets are mere pinpoints on a map the size of *Texas*, and hazards are even smaller. Navigational maps can only do so much, so a person has to fly blind. As fast as these ships are flying, a rock the size of a man's fist can completely destroy an *enormous* spaceship. At the separation point, the four groups veer away from each other in perfect unison, like a flower opening its petals, each headed for different quadrants of the planet. Flying just beyond the speed of light allows them to outrun the Gray's sensor returns... in theory. Spreading father apart, each freighter veers away from the ships in its group. In the last seconds, each freighter pulls hard on its *reverse engines* and drops them into normal space, just above the Reticulan's home-world of Reticuli.

It is a peaceful, bluish-green world. While Venus is Earth's *evil* twin, Reticuli is Earth's TRUE twin. If it weren't for the continents looking so different, Reticuli would be identical to Earth. The other freighters drop out of hyperspace above the planet; reflecting the sunlight, and looking like tiny flecks of silver. The tranquility lasts only for a moment. As if the Reticulans were ready for the arrival of humans, enemy star-fighters unleash a fury of weapons. The human attack ships spring out of the freighters' bellies and into a firestorm of enemy fire, like a mass of fireworks exploding at the same time. Freighters and attack ships alike take *massive* punishment. One ship launches many of its warheads, the white plumes streak toward the surface. Enemy ships destroy many missiles before concentrating their fire on the teardrop-shaped vessel.

Using a combination of energy weapons and railguns, the enemy star-fighters RIP into the nearest attack ship it can find, making it look like it was made of tissue paper. A hundred miles from any other human ships, it launches all of its nuclear warheads in all directions...except one. Moments later, the attack ship *explodes* in a bright flash of light. The blast instantly vaporizes the attack ship in an incredible nuclear explosion. A horizontal, blue shock wave originates from the vaporized vessel, and the circular shock wave expands *rapidly* through space. The blue shock wave demolishes a *dozen* enemy ships as it grows, taking them out of the fight... if they are that lucky. At the time, it seemed foolish for the human ship to the wildly fire its missiles, but now the logic becomes clear. The planet's gravity slowly takes hold of the wildly fired missiles, becoming both their navigation systems and their thrusters. Untouched by enemy weapons, one hundred of the deadly nuclear missiles move slowly toward the planet. The planet's gravity innocently pulls them downwards, and seals its own fate.

Despite losing *many* individual ships, the human attack fleet spreads around the planet, like oil over water. Spinning slowly, the attack ships launch nuclear missile after nuclear missile at the planet. Seconds later, the first missile lands its punch. A flash and 'smoke' follow in a beautiful, growing round pattern. Beautiful when seen from space, this is. Other missiles reach the surface as well, and growing round patterns erupt dot the planet's surface. The 'smoke' from the circles collide with each other and creates new patterns. Are the new flashes missiles, lightning or the beginnings of a nuclear firestorm? No longer a bluish-green and Earth-like, the planet is now charred and hellish, like a sooty version of Venus.

Some attack ships are completely free from harm, while others are not so fortunate. Without short-range weapons, the attack ships continue to suffer *ferocious* assaults even after the nuclear missiles are gone. Many captains have learned to keep one or two nuclear missiles in reserve, to try detonating them close to their own ship or to use one on themselves.

Mercifully free of the ferocious assaults, Colonel Decker watches the battle on the first attack ship's view-screen. The co-pilot walks up to him. "The Beta-Four freighter didn't arrive," he announces.

Decker seems indifferent, "That's why we fly side-by-side, and not single-file," he answers. "By flying side-by-side we don't *all* crash, if *one* of us crashes into something. Flying Finger-Four Formations won't help us, either. We're bending space-time back and forth, not making ripples in air. It will mess us up. We traveled *thirty-two* light years, and there are a lot things floating in space. Some are tiny, and some are not so tiny, but space is *so immense* that the risks are minute. Accidents *do* happen, though. On average, one percent of spaceships will crash into something for every 2.1 light years they travel, so we should have lost *four* freighters. We could easily take that as a sign that we're doing the right thing."

"How do we know this was the right planet?" the co-pilot asks, as if desperate for a good answer. "Or if all of it was even true?"

The pilot had started to turn to the view-screen, but stops. "It's a little late to be asking *those* questions," he responds.

The co-pilot looks down, "I know," he says. "I know we're 'just following orders,' and we shouldn't question any order, but I also feel like these are questions that should be asked."

The pilot takes a deep breath. "You are not alone," he says. "I asked my C/O those same questions, and you know what he told me?"

"What?" he sheepishly asks.

With the best poker face he could muster, Decker tells him, "He said, 'Harwell is our president, and we should never question him.'"

Amazed, Wells gasps. "Oh my God!" he bellows. "He actually *said* that?" He shakes his head. "And this guy is a Commanding Officer??"

Decker had tried to keep a straight face, but bursts out laughing at this point. Something in the tactical display catches his eye, though, diverting his attention. Preoccupied with the enemy's movements, his smile fades. "They are doing really dangerous maneuvers," he says, "and only a few are living through them." Wells gets quiet, and walks to the screen. "The Reticulans are not fighting for life," Decker tells him. "We've taken away any hope of *ever* landing again. They *know* they will die soon, and they don't want us to ever land again, either. There is no need for caution or restraint, since they're *already* dead. Why *not* fight as hard as they possibly can?"

Wells takes a deep breath, and lets it out. "Man, " he says, "Sometimes this job…" He shakes his head.

Decker cuts him off. "I know," he says. "I know. *Usually* military life is good: You train, you help other people and you get to shoot bad guys. But ethical boundaries tend to get crossed when you're the White House's bitch. We'll just follow the orders of the guy that's in the White House right now, and later we'll have a few drinks back at this pub I know.

In a year's time, we'll be settled on a new planet with a few *hundred* acres to ourselves."

Wells looks at him. "You really think it'll be that easy?"

Decker sits back in his chair, "That's what L'lith says."

"I don't trust her," he says.

Decker scratches his chin. "I understand where you're coming from," he says. "I doubt we'll get everything we want, but I think we'll get enough out of this thing, to make it worth it. I'm sure she's not doing all this just for generosity's sake."

Wells shakes his head again, "Mentally, she can run circles around President Harwell..."

Decker cuts him off. "But not General Hamilton," he says, finishing his statement. "He's a sharp cookie." Wells nods. Decker looks at the view-screen again. "We were a *lot* luckier than some of these poor bastards," he says. "It looks like all of our missiles have launched now. Let's head back to our freighter."

Many elected people swear an Oath of Office to protect to defend the U.S. Constitution before taking office. Honor kept politicians honest in the past, but that's not always true for the present. Such an oath should be <u>mortally binding</u> in the present. Honorable actions would be protected while unconstitutional actions would, and should, be considered treason. After a trial and if convicted, the traitor's execution should take place within **one** *year. Images work better than words, and that image would strongly deter any other would-be-traitors.*

Chapter 17

The Fiery Shield

As G'brael's shuttle flies frantically back to Earth, a bright red star appears. Growing larger as it approaches, the ship... K'kul's ship, has heard their call for help. A medical team meets them in the landing bay. G'brael is unconcious and covered in blood. "This happened at a construction site!" one doctor yells. "He probably has internal injuries, as well!" They rush him to the ship's medical facility.

Asher and Percival wait. Hours seem like days, and after a long while, K'kul walks to where Percival and Asher are waiting. "He's gone," K'kul tells them. Asher has only met G'brael twice, but feels tremendous sorrow at his death. He bows his head as his heart sinks, as though an unseen thread weights it. After several moments, K'kul speaks again. "G'brael spoke of a Drakyyn," he says. "Do either of you know what he was talking about?"

Percival replies first. "They were before my time," he replies. "He never mentioned anything to me."

K'kul sits on a chair across from the pair. "Probably an old memory," he says, then thinks and considers for a moment if G'brael meant something else.

Asher looks at the two of them. "What is a Drakyyn?" he asks.

Awakening from his thoughts. "They're gone now, but the Drakyyn were monstrous reptilian creatures," K'kul begins. "Long before humans came along, reptiles were the most evolved creatures in the galaxy. G'brael called them 'the latest models until humans came along.'" He smiles at the memory of his friend. "Pride led to jealousy. The Drakyyn came to Earth, even though they hadn't developed space travel, from the Sirius star group in the Orion constellation.

We have some ideas, but no one ever found *evidence* of how they got to Earth. They only had airplanes. They seem to have disguised themselves as human-like beings, because they told the ancient Sumerians that they created Mankind in their image. The Drakyyn used humans as slaves for a while but were repeatedly shamed by human mental abilities... and jealously eventually led to violence. They killed many, many people... including loved ones." K'kul stops for a minute, like he is reliving an event that happened several millennia ago. He takes a deep breath. "I'm sorry," he says. "I'm fine. I'm fine. A certain amount of emotion comes with the memory of the day my people died so needlessly."

Asher feels sorrow for him but is puzzled at the same time. He whispers to Percival, "I thought we were G'brael's people."

"He and G'brael are brothers," Percival whispers back.

K'kul takes a breath. "Yes," he says. "I knew I had one, but I didn't know who it was for a long time." He looks somewhat embarrassed. "I was still living in Puma Punku when I first tried teaching the people living in the middle of the Americas. They were very primitive when I arrived and it went fairly well. They weren't as primitive when I left, but they deified me anyway." He shakes his head. "Very embarrassing. I left and took an assembly of my people to a more northern group of people." Asher nods. "They were even more primitive. My brethren and I tried to teach them as well as we could, but they were so intent on symbols and deities..." He shakes his head again. "I thought a group of us would have more success, but..." He shakes his head again. "I gave up after that. I went back to Puma Punku to help me make sense of my failure. It takes *generation* after *generation* to slowly bring a culture up to speed. The process can't progress too quickly, or it will fail. The passage of time will do the same thing. We never went back."

The wheels in Asher's brain turn, "Wait a minute. White hair, white beard, Indians don't have beards, blue eyes, white skin, deity, teacher from the sea... You're Kukulcan!"

K'kul sits up in his chair. "That was a long time ago," he says in a low voice.

Asher can't sit still, so he stands. "This is so cool!" he chatters. "The girls are going to *love* this! I should have seen it sooner. I *thought* your name sounded familiar!" He stops for a moment. "Wait a minute," he says, looking at K'kul's face. "I thought you were supposed to have a big head or something," he says, putting his hand over his head as if clutching a pretend head.

"Yes," he says. "We were wearing rings on the *outside* of our heads in those days, so I wore a type of hat to cover it. They had never seen a hat with a 'crown' before and thought I had a big head. Primitive people don't understand what you and I take for granted." He sighs. "That was one of my biggest mistakes. The Spanish wore 'large-crowned' hats and even modified the armor of their Conquistador's armor to exploit my mistake. Human cleverness is a double-edged sword, and the Maya paid the price. Deeper into North America, the American Indians had never seen a horse before, so when they saw the Conquistadors on horseback, they thought they were one creature."

The wheels in Asher's brain kept spinning. "One of the last things that G'brael talked about was deceiving the Osirians. He didn't get to finish. Do you know what he was talking about?"

K'kul sits back in his chair. "Yes," he says in a deep voice. He takes a very deep breath and releases it before he begins. "L'lith is a serpent, the queen of all serpents. We thought President Harwell saw through her lies and made the Osirians work for *you*."

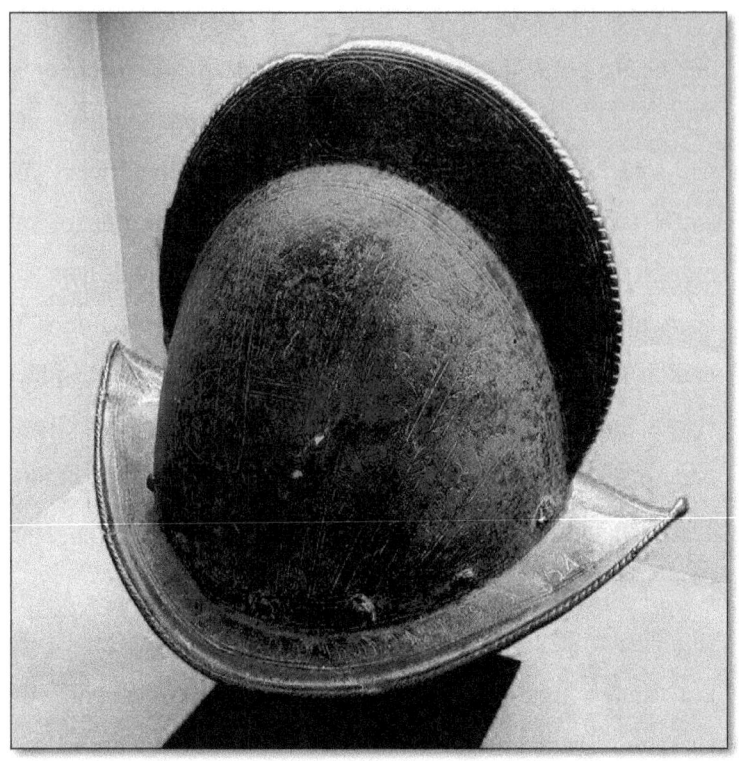

Asher laughs. "That's not likely."

Percival comes back with, "We know that *now*. "Your country's, even your world's political systems, are heavily infested with serpents, even though your world's and your country's *people* are not. I don't see how your country has lasted as long as it has.

"Serpents LIE," K'kul injects. The two other men look at him. "They lie about who and what they are. That's how they get into positions of power."

Looking back at Asher, "Yes," Percival says. "For the longest time we thought that you knew that whole 'global warming'/'climate change' thing was a lie."

"You mean it's not true?" he asks.

Percival just groans. K'kul waves the back of his hand like he's shooing a fly from his face. "Not in the least," K'kul answers. "I'd rather not tell you what I *really* think of it. We thought you had figured it out centuries ago. You had closed the door on an Ice Age... and then this one serpent comes along!" He sighs heavily, resigning himself. "Of course, do you think a serpent will actually tell you the *truth*?!"

Asher is lost for words. "Well..."

K'kul cuts him off. "Sorry," he says. "Rhetorical question," he says. "Serpents lie about who they are and what they want. Oh, they speak the truth when it serves their purposes or when they're being stupid." He leans toward Asher and pretends to whisper. "And they can definitely BE STUPID." He points to his head. "They aren't very bright to begin with. This one and others like him, convinced the world that 'the planet has a temperature' and that carbon dioxide is a pollutant." Asher doesn't comment. He just listens. *"In fact,"* he roars, "the Little Ice Age never ended. The carbon dioxide has been keeping the Ice Age *at bay* for the last 160 years! It takes more and more to keep it at bay, but once you hit a certain point… You were doing it." He smiles. "A decrease *now* means that the Little Ice Age will catch up. This was a very bad time for him to do this. He has doomed *himself,* along with everyone else."

Asher's heart skips a beat, "We can fix it," he says, almost panicked. "I can tell the president how important…"

K'kul cuts him off. "It's too late," he says quietly, shaking his head. "Carbon dioxide needs *time* to dissolve in the ocean, then be used by the plankton. No," he says, patting Asher's leg, "It has been *just* a deception so a few serpents can get rich. It's that simple." He sighs. "Throughout most of 5th Commencement history, rich men got rich off the backs of other men. The Golden Rule was 'He who has the gold makes the rules.' The invention of capitalism changed all that. Everyone makes money, so labor is voluntary. It wasn't that way before. Capitalists can lose *huge* sums of money… or gain huge sums of money. It's a gamble. Serpents talk about the 'evils of making money' but they never mention the amount of work it takes, the lives it enriches…" He looks directly at Asher, "or the severity of the risks these people take. Some people will stop at *nothing* to destroy another person's happiness, no matter how insignificant that happiness. It could be cheap gasoline, a cold air conditioner, the lack of malaria or even cupcakes in school." He grins at the last one. "They want to bring back the old ways. They will help each other, if it serves their purposes or cannibalize each other, if it serves their purposes. These people remind us of the Drakyyn, FILLED with anger, spite and venom; eager to hurt and even to kill humans. That's why we call them *serpents*."

Asher shakes his head. "We're safe," he says. "Someone that vile and destructive would have gone to jail a long time ago."

"They hide," Percival says.

"They're good at hiding... and often in plain sight," K'kul adds. "They usually take mundane jobs, but narcissism is another common trait. They might take a job in politics or higher education. You might not even realize what they're doing unless you watch them. Terrorism doesn't require bravery and they don't have any. Terrorists like them don't expose themselves to the light of truth. They hide like cockroaches. Change their names. Tell people friendly words while *quietly* subverting your society. Most people cannot fathom the anger and the venom that these people feel toward Mankind, but also they can't fathom the depths of your own oceans or the size of their own sun or the distance to the *very next* star."

Asher changes the subject and tries to distance himself. "We ended slavery in this country 152 years ago."

K'kul simply nods his head, "Serpents want to bring it back," he says. "A noble gesture on your part, but American slavery was the kindest in all of 5th Commencement history."

Asher gawks at him. "Really?!" he asks in shock. "Are you *serious*?"

K'kul calmly turns his head. "Oh yes," he answers. "Like I said, things were different in the past, and America was one of the *last* countries to have slavery, not the first. Men got rich from the forced labor of other men. Mining wasn't the most well known user of slaves, but it was the most common. Mines were exceedingly dangerous at the time, and slaves were cheap. Most slaves died within two years. Not all, but most. It might be copper, lead, cinnabar or something even worse. The more difficult the mining process, the higher the price. Mining was done by hand and there was certainly nothing to keep the dust out of a slave's lungs. That's why a rich man couldn't get into Heaven. It wasn't the money. It was how he MADE the money. America changed all that. Most Americans of the past had a deep understanding of the

Bible, while many Americans of the present lack that understanding. The Bible is very good at building a person's ability to empathize with other people."

Again, Asher tries to distance himself. "The American government helps its people to feel more emotion for each other."

K'kul shakes his head. "Empathy and emotion are not the same thing. Emotion is a primitive brain function and empathy is a high brain function. You're being dumbed-down and don't even realize it. Americans of the *past*, however, more than anyone else in 5th Commencement history, saw slaves as people. Ironically, black slavery was started by a black man. A few slave-owners would hurt a slave, just for fun, but the vast majority of Americans would *not*. In all of 5th Commencement history, America had the only slave population that actually *grew*. President Lincoln didn't recognize this and tried to change things 'the wrong way.' More than 600,000 American citizens paid for his mistake."

Asher jumps to his feet. "They started it by firing on Fort Sumter!"

He didn't move. "Fort Sumter was empty," he replies.

Asher stops and stares at K'kul. "Empty?" he asks and slowly sits down again.

"Practically," he replies. "The governor warned them, the commanding officer warned them and then they spent two days slow-shelling the fort. No one died, there was no blaze, the fort was completely within the borders of the state and it had no strategic value. Any other president might have called it 'vandalism,' but Lincoln called it 'war.'" He leans back in his chair, interlacing his fingers. Sighing heavily, "Several generations later, there is still an issue between the states. Isn't there?" he says. His question sounds like a statement. Asher is lost for words. There *is* an issue. He knows the answer, but can't bring himself to say it.

K'kul doesn't have that problem. "Your country needs a divorce," he says flatly. Asher is still stunned. "Bigger isn't always better," he tells him. "Split into more than two countries this time. Having two sides never works. One side always overpowers the other. I suggest splitting into large regions, let *those* become countries and let the smaller regions become states. That way you can do what you want, they can do what they want and no one drags anyone down."

He sighs again and his 'calm demeanor' slips into a 'reminiscent demeanor.' "Europe was *perfectly* positioned to outperform America."

Asher jumps in. "Europeans found the 'god particle!' he announces. "G'brael said it didn't exist."

224

Percival answers. "Europe is infested with serpents," he says.

"Yes!" K'kul concurs. "Do you really expect a serpent to tell you the truth?!" he asks and says, "It's another lie!" "Someone who lies isn't necessarily a serpent, but *all* serpents lie. Germany introduced Europe to socialism during your Second World War and turned many Europeans into serpents. They've taken a foothold in your country as well. Leaders can speed it up or slow it down, but bureaucracies are the real danger!" He throws up his hands. "Communism will take Europe!" he says in defeat. "The French will lead all of Europe, with the Germans kicking and screaming. Many Germans *know* what it's like to live under a dictator's thumb. The French have not felt that helplessness in dozens of generations. They've forgotten about the starvation, the disease, the needless deaths and the conscription," he tells him. K'kul talks about it like an old memory. "The French say, 'No. It won't happen to *me!*' Then it does. Young Frenchmen," he says, "*ripped* from their families... only to die in pointless wars in foreign countries."

Asher finds his voice. "Napoleon?" he asks.

"Yes," he answers. "Emperors, kings and dictators, power-hungry men searching for land, power and the perfect warrior to give it to them." He leans over to him. "Your Sasquatch came from that search."

Asher laughs. "How IN THE WORLD are those two related?" he asks, almost daring him to answer.

"He is the perfect warrior," K'kul says flatly. "Very tall, extremely strong and extraordinarily stealthy." Asher's smile slowly fades. "What you call 'Bigfoot' was an experimental failure many, many years ago. Each Commencement of Mankind has had breeding programs, one city-state competing against another. That's why versions of Sasquatch live on most of your continents. They wanted super-warriors: Extremely tall and extremely strong warriors for their armies. They bred the tallest of their people and added ape DNA to get their strength. It was well structured and had very little cross breeding... at first. Emotion and arrogance got in the way. Once the inbreeding started... Well, there just weren't enough of them to maintain a 'normal' intelligence level." He sighs. "Hairy, nine-foot tall people with the strength of an elephant and the IQ of a small child don't fit well into civilized society. They were ridiculed in the cities, so they made homes in the forests, away from other humans. Sasquatches are sentient beings but only understand the world the way a small child understands it. They are quite at home in the forests, though. They know it so well that finding them is like finding a Native

American tracker." He shakes his head and laughs. "Good luck! You'll need technology to find them!"

Asher smiles. "I've always thought that something like Sasquatch was fairly likely, but as time goes on and we still haven't found any proof... I have my doubts we'll *ever* find him."

K'kul chuckles. "And you never will," he says. "As long as you keep paying crooks to search for him, they'll keep letting you pay them. The moment they succeed is the moment 'the money train' stops. Oh, there's an honest Sasquatch tracker every now and then... and Sasquatch has been found many times. These honest people don't want to say that they've found him, because he is so human... and they know what would happen to him if they did. Just walk a tracking dog through the woods, find some footprints, have the dog sniff the footprints, then go find the one that made them."

Asher throws his hands up and cuts him off in mid-stride. "Whoa!" he barks. "How is using a dog the same thing as using technology?"

Percival answers, "'Technology' doesn't mean 'only electronics.' It's just a fancy word for 'tools'."

K'kul nods in agreement, and Asher grudgingly accepts the answer. "As I was saying, if you want to speed up the process, tether several balloons each having a microphone to a several very-far-apart trees and wait for one of his 'calls.' They make very distinct and loud calls. Triangulate it, just like a GPS, then use a tracking dog. But keep in mind that killing one of them is a very, *very* bad idea. Remember they were originally designed to be super-warriors... that trait hasn't disappeared. They may not be smart, but they *know* stealth. A few deer rifles are no match against wave after wave of angry and *cunning* nine-foot-tall men, each with the strength of an elephant. Many people have eight-foot ceilings. Sasquatches are taller than that. It's much safer to use video and infrared video. Use them at the same time but not in the same footage."

Introspective again. "L'lith is like one those power-hungry kings," he says. "She used geological heat to power a very large weapon. It backfired and melted the polar ice caps, which were *much* larger in those days. The Earth's sea level rose and Atlantis, being an island, disappeared under a mile of water.

Asher suddenly goes white-faced and looks at K'kul. "Oh crap!" he says and jumps to him feet. "I just remembered. L'lith set us up!"

K'kul chuckles again. "Of course she did," K'kul says. "I told you she's the *queen* of serpents!"

He shakes his head. "No. It's worse than that," he says. "She tricked President Harwell into taking the world's nuclear weapons and attacking one of the Reticulan's home-worlds."

K'kul smile instantly disappears. "Only one?" he asks. Asher nods. K'kul stands up, saying, "They've got eleven more. They'll counterattack and..." he gasps and whirls around, "and you're defenseless."

Asher nods. "I realized her plan right after G'brael got hurt."

K'kul has a desperate look on his face. "This is bad," he says. "You don't mess with the Reticulans, and you certainly don't attack them! Call the White House and tell them what's going on! We need to get as many of your people off the planet as quickly as we can! The counter-attack may already be on its way!"

*Fluoride **in water** does NOT help teeth. Although many compounds are called 'fluoride,' all of them contain the deadly element fluorine. Josef Stalin used fluoride in Soviet concentration camps and in East Germany to increase obedience to Soviet authority. Fluoride leaches into some water supplies and has been artificially added to others since the 1940s. In 1961, Dr. Stanley Milgram did his now-infamous research on 'Obedience to Authority.' He found that 65% of people would electrocute another person if an authority figure instructed. Fluoride's effects increase with time, and Milgram's experiments have been repeated since then. As suspected, civil obedience is much higher today.*

Chapter 18

The Counter-Attack

The White House's switchboard eventually routes Asher's call to General Hamilton. "No, Mr. Asher," he says on the phone. "I cannot. President Harwell removed me from that position."

"Can you tell him something, then?" he asks.

"I'll do what I can, Mr. Asher. What is the message?"

He pauses for a second. "It was a trap, General. L'lith betrayed us," he tells him. General Hamilton closes his eyes and takes a deep breath. "General?" he asks.

"Yes, Mr. Asher," he says. "I'm here. I was afraid of something like this. What's going on?"

"L'lith tricked President Harwell into attacking a Reticulan home-world with all of Earth's nuclear weapons," he says.

"The Grays?" the general asks.

Asher nods and says, "Yes." "They have *twelve* planets, General, not just one. And Reticulans are just like Africanized bees, they fight and fight and fight until they're dead. We're defenseless."

He motions to a young soldier, who immediately brings him a notepad. "I was afraid of something like this," he says, starting to write. "When something seems to good to be true, it probably is. How much time do we have?" he asks.

"We don't know," Asher tells him. "Have any messages come from the fleet, yet?"

He whispers to the soldier again, who quickly goes to another room. "Yes," the general replies. "We heard from them about 45 minutes ago. They took casualties, but successfully delivered their entire arsenal. Reticuli is a mere cinder now."

The soldier runs back to the general, salutes him and reports. "Sir, there's no answer from the fleet," he says, almost frantic. "The soldiers monitoring that 'ansible thing' that L'lith gave us, said that there was chatter every now and then, but there hasn't been anything else for the last 23 minutes. They thought it was just 'radio silence' until we tried to contact them just now." He gulps. "There's no answer."

"Thank you, Son," General Hamilton tells him, salutes and talks to Asher. "Did you hear all of that?" he asks.

Asher's lifts his head, which had fallen to the control panel when he heard the news. "Yes," he answers. "Loud and clear, General."

"There's no reason to jump to conclusions," he says. "It could be a glitch on our end or their end. I'm sure all those nukes going off has some side effects."

Asher nods, even though no one can see him. "You're right, General," he says, with knots in his stomach. "I'll get as much intel as I can and contact you again in just a few minutes." K'kul walks up to him. "H... Hold on, General." His body language answers the question. "ALL of them?!" Asher gasps.

"I'm sorry," K'kul tells him. "L'lith put sensors around the star system to let other races know that the attack didn't come from the Osirians. We got that information, also. Fifteen minutes ago, the sensors recorded an enormous enemy fleet appeared out of hyperspace and destroyed your entire fleet in less than 30 seconds. There was no time for a distress call."

Asher's heart sinks further. "I guess that answers *that* question," he mutters.

"That enemy fleet will come *here* next," K'kul says. "You have to get as many people off the Earth as fast as you can."

"Mars is nearly ready for people to move-in," Asher tells the general. "I didn't understand why General P'al put humans underground and behind bars, but now I do. They want the few of us that survive this attack to continue to exist. I'm not sure why, yet."

K'kul answers. "You are the greatest Commencement of Mankind in galactic history. You are gods to the rest of the galaxy... even higher than L'lith herself. Your survival, even if in a cage, gives her the right to rule over the *entire* galaxy."

Asher stares at K'kul for a moment. "We... We'll be there in..."

"Ten minutes," K'kul tells him.

"Gather as many people as you can, General," Asher tells him. "Mankind's survival depends on this! We'll be there in ten minutes."

The phone in General Hamilton's suddenly seems heavier. He hangs up the phone and sighs. "Is this what the Mayan Calendar predicted?"

Glossary

February, 1882 – Nicola Tesla has his greatest epiphany… alternating current

April 14, 1912 – *R.M.S. Titanic* struck a large inceberg, and sank 4 hours later

December 14, 1940 – plutonium was first created in Berkeley, California

February 25, 1942 – The Battle of Los Angeles

ACU – Anti-aircraft unit. A permanent weapons emplacement used to destroy aerial targets.

Ansible – /an SIH buhl/ - 'Radio' used for interstellar communications. Instantaneous communicator.

Amoeba Effect – common phenomenon where people in the same area, think and act alike

Anunnaki – /ah noo NAH kee/ - aliens/gods that told the ancient Sumerians that the Anunnaki created all Mankind

Ares /AIR eez/

    1.   Greek god of war (Mars in Roman mythology)

    2.   The name of the large Osirian transport/storage ship

Aristocles – /ah RIS toh klees/ - the given name of Plato. He wrote a few things about Atlantis, but suddenly stopped - almost in mid-sentence.

Atlantis – an ancient city that was destroyed by a flood thousands of years ago, but rebuilt underwater

Atlanteans – /at LAN tee uhz/ - Citizens of Atlantis

Aurora – /uh ROHR uh/ - the alleged name of a very fast and secret, American-made aircraft

Aurora Borealis – the Northern Lights

Battle of Los Angeles, The – Not a movie or a music album. February 25, 1942. Although it was called 'wartime jitters' by people that weren't there to see it, hundreds of people (including an admiral) said that it actually happened.

Beowulf – /BAY oh wulf/

    1.   The hero of the *Beowulf* heroic epic poem

    2.   An anonymously-written Anglo-Saxon heroic epic poem. It was written about the 8th Century A.D., set in Scandinavia.

Breaking foul – In the game of pool (billiards), a foul committed at the break (first play) in which at least three balls must bounce off a side rail. Also called a 'bad break.'

Cambrian Explosion – /KAME bree uhn/ - the name given for the extremely sudden and massively diverse appearance of animal life on Earth. It happened in both fresh and salt water, from 542 million years ago to 488 million years ago

Captain T'rell – /TAH rel/ - Osirian army (Cherubim) captain that works for L'lith in the White House

Charnia – /char NEE uh/ - a fern frond-like animal from the Cambrian period of the Paleozoic era

Cherubim - /CHAIR oo bihm/

1. The Osirian army

2. The 2nd Order of angels; they aren't angelic

Chitin – /KI tin/ - a tough, semitransparent substance forming the principal component of arthropod exoskeletons; prior to the evolution of bone, it also formed arthropod endoskeletons

Cinnabar - /SIN uh bahr/ - Mercury ore. It is highly toxic, and often found as a red crystal and crushed into dust.

Commencement of Mankind – one of the five 'eras' of humanity. This one is the fifth.

Council of Nine – a council made up of the nine leaders of the nine underwater city-states

Crown of a Hat – the portion of a hat covering the top of the head; usually somewhat rigid and gives the appearance that the wearer's head is larger than it appears

Cue ball – in the game of pool (billiards), the solid white ball that the player strikes

Dark Energy – In astronomy, the theoretical energy that grows between the galaxies, causing them to spread apart. This is used to explain the expansion of the universe.

Dark Matter – In astronomy, an object of *any* size that does not emit light (e.g. asteroid, planetoid, burned-out star, black hole, etc.) The definition has come to include both matter and *theoretical* matter.

Diamagnetic – A non-magnetic substance that tends to follow a very strong or a very large magnetic field (like the Earth's field). This is why the sea level is higher on one side of the Panama Canal that the other.

Drakyyn – /drah KEE ehn/ - a reptilian race from the Sirius star group. They felt jealousy and hate toward Mankind, so they killed as many humans as possible. They were thought to be extinct, but that isn't true.

Ejecta – the magma, rock, ground and pyroclastic ash that is dislodged & ejected when a volcano erupts

Emotion – A feeling. It comes from the amygdala, in the primitive area of the brain.

Empathy – The ability to relate to another person's situation, from their point-of-view. Although it's often confused with feelings, but it comes from a higher part of the brain. This moral part of the brain is turned-off in psychopaths.

Epiphany – moment of brilliant insight

Exasperated – Frustrated

Federal government – A form of government that bands sovereign states together. A federal government can form treaties and do a few other things, on the behalf of all the states, and divides power among different people. It is also called a federation.

Finger-Four Formation – A flight formation, based on the V shape of a flock of birds, but adapted to fighter airplanes. It is a formation of four airplanes: 1 to the right of the lead plane, and 2 to its left. It is not to be confused with the 'Missing Man Formation,' but is named for a man's fingertips. When numerous groups of these formations are linked, it is called a 'Finger-Four Squadron.'

Fort Sumter – A fortification located in Charleston Harbor in Charleston, South Carolina. Although construction began after The War of 1812, the project was abandoned for nearly forty years, when Abraham Lincoln came into power. It is best known as the 'spark' that started the American Civil War.

FTL – Faster Than Light travel

G'brael – /guh BREE ahl/ - Leader of Atlantis and Council of Nine member

Garuda – /guh ROO duh/ - a large, mythical bird-like creature flown by Vishnu, the supreme God in the Vaishnavite tradition of Hinduism

General P'al – /PAH ahl/ - The Osirian Supreme Commander. He is very tall, speaking with strange grammar and extremely short sentences. He also has an abnormally deep voice and hides a dangerous secret.

God particle – the Higgs Boson

Grays – an alien species from the Reticuli star group

Grendel – /GREN duhl/

1. The character, antagonist, in epic poem *Beowulf*

2. A modern literary work, written in conjunction to the epic poem *Beowulf*, but from the antagonist's point of view

Hephaes – /HI fayz/ - (Both singular and plural) Osirian construction robots. While they look like mannequins that can move, some are human-sized, and some are 150 feet tall.

Hephaestus – /hi FEST uhs/ - Greek god of forging and manufacturing (Vulcan in Roman mythology)

Heron (of Alexandria) – /HAIR uhn/ - a very gifted ancient Greek engineer. He is often associated with Alexandia, Egypt – the location of the Great Library. One of his many inventions was the aeolipile, a steam-powered device similar to a modern steam engine. Somehow a genius like him didn't think to use this device to start the Industrial Revolution back in the 1st century AD.

Higgs Boson – In particle physics, the theoretical sub-atomic particle that gives other sub-atomic particles their mass.

Horn of a continent – NOT a musical instrument; it is a headland; an island marking the extreme tip of a continent, extending into a large body of water (it often looks like a large, round object sticking out of the water)

Hurricane Katrina – a large hurricane that hit New Orleans, Louisiana, in 2005. The levies broke and the city flooded, killing many people.

Jim Crow Laws – mainly in the southern United States from 1877 to the mid-1960s, laws that restricted the rights of black people and made them into second-class citizens

Johnson, Anthony – A freed black indentured servant who convinced a 17th Century Virgina court that his own indentured servant, a fellow black man, should be enslaved. This marked the beginning of American slavery.

K'kul – /kuh KOOL/ - Council of Nine member, and brother of G'brael

K'ler – /KAH ler/ - Osirian instructor, teaching anti-gravitational flight and FTL physics

Kammler, Hans – SS brigadier general, Roman Catholic and head of ALL of Nazi Germany's Black (Secret) Projects. Besides Hitler, he was the only man that knew about them all. He disappeared after the war. Although several people swear to his death, there are five versions of that death. He probably didn't die at all.

Karate Gi – a light and loose-fitting karate training uniform

Kubla Khan – /KOO bluh • KAHN/

1. The 13th century Mongolian ruler and emperor of China

2. A poem written by Samuel Taylor Coleridge in 1797 (published in 1816), after an opium-induced vision

Kukulcan – /koo kool KAHN/ - a white-haired, white-bearded, Caucasian man ascribed by the ancient Maya as teaching them and then leaving to live in the sea

Kukulkan – /koo kool KAHN/ - The snake deity of the ancient Maya and it means "feathered serpent." Called Q'uq'umatz of the K'iche' Maya and to Quetzalcoatl to the Aztecs. It takes its name from thr mythical teacher Kukulcan.

Leviathan – a very large ship

L'lith – /LAH lith/ - Leader of Osiria and Council of Nine member

Lilith – /LIL uth/ - from the Christian Bible, the Jewish Torah and the Islamic Koran. The first wife of Adam. She disobeyed God and was banned from the Garden of Eden. Enraged, she merged with a demon and became a scourge on Mankind. A succubus.

Lilith Abi – /LIL uth • UH bi/ - a Hebrew phrase meaning, "Lilith be gone," inscribed on amulets protecting a child from Lilith. She is accused of causing Sudden Infant Death Syndrome in Lilith's attempts to kill 100 children per night. Scholars believe it is the origin of the world *lullaby*.

Little Ice Age – period between 1300 AD and 1850 AD that was much colder than normal. Snow and ice were *very* common.

Long Count – The long version of the Mayan calendar, and the combination of two smaller calendars. It is a complicated, but extremely accurate, way of counting days.

Lunar Month – time period equal to 27.3 Earth days

Lunar Year – time period equal to one lunar month

M'kul – /muh KOOL/ - a Council of Nine Member

Magnetic north pole – An imaginary concept, and a convenient coincidence. Since magnets align themselves very close to Earth's rotational North Pole, so that is used for navigation.

Mahabharata – /mah hah BAR uh tuh/ - one of the two major Sanskrit epics of ancient India. It's a narrative of the Kurukshetra War, philosophical material and the story of Damayanti.

Maya – /MI yuh/ - Meso-american Indians inhabiting southeast Mexico, Guatemala and Belize. Their civilization lasted for 1,500 years and reached its height between 300 and 900 AD, before being destroyed by the Spanish Conquistadors in mid-16th century. The Maya are noted for their architecture, city planning, mathematic skills, calendar and their hieroglyphic writing system.

Mohendro Daro – /moh HEN droh • DAR oh/ - a city in ancient Pakistan that shows evidence of intense heat and radiation, as if it had been the site of a nuclear explosion thousands of hears ago

Molluscs – freshwater and marine animals from the Cambrian period of the Paleozoic era. They are still alive today in the form of clams and oysters.

Mount Tambora – a supervolcano in Indonesia. It erupted in early April of 1815, causing the infamous 'Year Without A Summer.'

Naga – /nah GAH/ according to the *Mahabharata* of ancient India, they were people with both human and serpent traits, and the deserving victims of a sacrifice to Garuda

National government – A single, sovereign government that governs a single nation. This is the typical form. The larger it gets (population), the more likely corruption flourishes.

Neural Omission – a method to remove a thought from a person's mind

Neutrino – /noo TREE noh/ - In particle physics, a theoretical sub-atomic particle that is electrically neutral and super-light (undetectable)

Olophagus – /oh loh FAY gus/ - Greek word meaning, "swallows whole." A dragon that terrorized medieval Poland.

Opabinia – /oh puh BIN ee uh/ - a marine animal with five eyes, a V-shaped tail and a trunk-like/mantis-like stalk, from the Cambrian period of the Paleozoic era

Order of Magnitude – Ten times whatever you're talking about. If something is twice as big, it's not even one order of magnitude, but if something is 1,000 times as big, then it's three orders of magnitude.

Osiria – /oh SEER ee uh/ - home of the enemy of ancient Atlantis. It was destroyed in ancient times, but rebuilt underwater. The Ancient Egyptians called it 'Osiris,' thought of it as a single person and worshipped it as a god. He is a green-skinned and bearded god of the underword. (Under the world)

PC – politically correct

Papal bull – /pay PUL • BUHL/ - a formal, written proclamation from the Pope (sealed with a leaden bulla)

Pauldron - /PAHL drahn/

1. When used with a cape, it is a leather guard that covers the shoulders, and holds the cape. This type is ceremonial, so it is usually symmetrical.
2. When used on plate armor, it is a steel guard that covers the shoulders. This type is for defense against right-handed attackers, so the pauldrons on each shoulder are *rarely* symmetically.
3. Sometimes both plate armor and a cape are used together.

Percival – A young, Scandinavian-looking Atlantean helmsman. He primarily works for K'kul, but occasionally for G'brael.

Permian Mass Extinction – A mass extinction that occurred 252.2 million years ago. (Caused by the Lemurian-Reticulan war.) It was the greatest mass extinction event in Earth's history. Also called the Periam-Triassic Extinction Event, and The Great Dying.

Phyla – /FI luh/ - Plural of the word 'phylum.' The 2nd level (of 7 levels) of biological classification: Kingdom, Phylum, Class, Order, Family, Genus and Species.

Pidima – /PID ee muh/ - Greek word meaning, "to bounce." Evasive maneuver that dodges incoming projectiles.

Pikaia – /pih KI uh/ - a marine animal from the Cambrian period of the Paleozoic era. Although it didn't have a well-defined head, it looked like a cross between a leech and a fish. It was one of the first animals to have a backbone.

Puma Punku – /POO muh • POON koo/ - A remarkably advanced archaeological site in Bolivia (central South America). The stones are extremely hard, while having deep and incredibly symmetric details. The stones also use a very sophisticated interlocking system. It was used for a long time, then destroyed by its own builders. The date of Puma Punku's construction is still hotly debated.

Quadrant – one-fourth of something

R'ma – /ruh MAH/ - a Council of Nine Member

Railgun – an electrically powered artillery gun that accelerates a conductive projectile along electromagnetic rails. It only uses electrical energy to propel the projectile, which travels *much* faster than firearm technology allows.

Rails – in the game of pool (billiards), the side wall of the tabletop

Reticulan – /re TIK yu Luhn/ - An alien. A Gray.

Reticuli – /re TIK yu lie/ - the Grays' home-world

Revolution – In physics, when something (a planet, for example) goes around something else (the sun, for example). It's also called an orbit.

Ring of Solomon – the old name for an angel's halo

RIO – /REE oh/ - Radio Intercept Officer. The navigator in a two-man military jet.

Rotation – when something spins in a circle (a planet, for example), like a top spins

Rotational North Pole – the extreme top of 'the invisible stick' upon which any planet rotates (not revolves)

S'lon – /suh LAHN/ - a human android of Atlantean design

SAM – /SAM/ - Surface-to-Air-Missile.

Schliemann, Heinrich – German amateur archaeologist who used Homer's epic, *Iliad*, to uncover the ancient city of Troy in 1868

Sentient – /sen TEE ent/ - consciousness or self-awareness

Serpent – A human of either gender, bent on harming other humans (plural). A human traitor to Mankind. They are reminiscent of the Drakyyn in the hatred they feel toward humans.

Shoot (a cue ball) – in the game of pool (billiards), striking the cue ball with a poolstick

Solar Year – time period equal to 365.25 Earth days

Sophist – /SOH fist/ - a "wise man" in ancient Greece. He is usually a teacher and/or an author.

Sporadically – occasionally

Stannum – /STAN num/ - a silvery alloy that is used both to significantly repel seawater from spaceships and to make anti-gravity generators

Stella Kowalski – one of the three main characters in Tennessee Williams' screenplay "A Streetcar Named Dessire". In the 1951 movie, Kim Hunter played her, alongside Marlon Brando and Vivien Leigh.

Supervolcano – A volcano capable of erupting more than 240 cubic *miles* of ejecta. There are only a handful of these in the world.

Telsa Coil – a doughnut-shaped, resonant transformer circuit (spark generator) invented by Nicola Tesla around 1891

Thectardis – /thek TAR dis/ - a marine animal from the Cambrian period of the Paleozoic era and looked like an inverted cone. It did not seem to attach to anything or dig, apparently preferring to 'move around' on the tip of its body and opposite of a snail.

Theropod – A three-toed, carnivorous dinosaur. There are the ancestors of modern birds.

Trilobite – /TRI loh bit/ - a marine animal, resembling a cross between a roly-poly bug and a horseshoe crab, from the Cambrian period of the Paleozoic era.

Troy – ancient city that was made famous by Homer's epic, *Iliad*, the Trojan War and the Trojan Horse

T. Rex (*Tyrannosaurus Rex*) – a carnivorous, Theropod dinosaur that lived between 67 million years ago and 65.5 million years ago, during the late Cretaceous Period

Umbra – The darkest part of a shadow. The penumbra and the antumbra being the other two parts.

Valles Marineris – An enormous valley on Mars, 2,500 miles long, 120 miles at it widest and 20,000 feet at its deepest, near the equator.

Vimina – /vee MAH nuh/

1. In ancient times, a wingless aerial craft made famous by the Indian epic, *Mahabharata*, the modern craft bears the same name

2. In modern times, a small aerial craft without wings, usually cigar-shaped and silver

Vishnu – /VISH noo/ - is the supreme God in the Vaishnavite tradition of Hinduism

Vitrification – /vih trih fih KAY shun/ - Conversion of rocky or clay substances into a glazed, glass-like material. It's usually done with extreme heat and somewhat resembles the effects of a kiln on ceramics, but to a much greater extent.

Whiteman Air Force Base – an Air Force base in Kansas City, Missouri, where most of the B-2 Stealth Bombers are based

Wow! Signal – in August of 1977, within 4 years of using the Big Ear radio telescope, scientists searching for an alien signal, detected a very intense interstellar radio signal that lasted for a full 72 seconds. Its origin (a small area in the Sagittarius Constellation) has been scanned many times, but the radio signal has vanished.

Year Without A Summer – The summer (actually the whole year) of 1816. During the Little Ice Age, the super-volcano, Mount Tambora in Indonesia, erupted in April of 1815. The global effect wasn't felt until 1816. Amidst crop failures, starvation and snow for an entire year; Mary Shelley wrote the book <u>Frankenstein</u>, rich with themes of ice and snow.

Yellowstone Caldera – A caldera (depression of a volcano's mouth) located in Yellowstone National Park. It is 34 miles by 45 miles.

Zeta-2 Reticuli – A white, main sequence star in the Reticulum constellation ("The Net"), and the companion star (a binary solar system) of Zeta-1 Reticuli. The star is remarkably similar to the Sun and has been suspected of having planets in 'The Habitable Zone.'

"If you tell a big enough lie and tell it frequently enough, it will be believed."

- Adolf Hitler

"By the skillful and <u>sustained</u> use of propaganda, one can make a people see even heaven as hell, or an extremely wretched life as paradise."

- Adolf Hitler

"What good fortune for governments that the people do not think."

- Adolf Hitler

"If you win, you need not have to explain...If you lose, you should not *be there* to explain!"

- Adolf Hitler

ABOUT THE AUTHOR

Matthew B. Thompson is a 35+ year Texas resident and an avid fan of science, science-fiction and history. He earned an Eagle Scout rank at a young age, but was stricken with a brain tumor shortly after earning a Bachelor of Science degree. After a short time in a wheelchair, he progressed to a walker and then to a cane… if anything at all. He is now married and a stay-at-home father for their small child.